In the Company of Angels

N. M. KELBY

IN THE COMPANY OF ANGELS

NEW YORK
An Imprint of Hyperion

Library of Congress Cataloging-in-Publication Data

Kelby, N.M.

    In the company of angels / by N.M. Kelby.—1st ed.

      p.   cm.

    ISBN 0-7868-6666-7

    1. World War, 1939-1945—Belgium—Fiction. 2. World War, 1939-1945—France—Fiction. 3. Holocaust, Jewish (1939-1945)—Fiction. 4. Jewish girls—Fiction. 5. Miracles—Fiction. 6. Belgium—Fiction. 7. France—Fiction. 8 Nuns—Fiction. I. Title.

    PS3561. E382 I5   2001

    813'.6—dc21   00-040873

Paperback ISBN 0-7868-8583-1

Book design by C. Linda Dingler

FIRST PAPERBACK EDITION

10 9 8 7 6 5 4 3 2 1

To my daughter, Hannah,

who,

through her death,

set forth miracles, redeemed faith,

and started me on this journey.

And to my husband, Steven, for all the rest.

1

Before the Germans bombed Belgium in 1940, Tournai was a city that creaked under the weight of its own rich history. Conquered by the French, it was thought more beautiful than Paris. Conquered by the English, it was the favored city of King Henry the Eighth.

It was also a city of God.

One hundred bell towers, four hundred bells. So many churches, their spires teetering at odd angles, they eclipsed the narrow streets, streets filled with knots of nuns and priests moving about like so many bees.

God was Tournai's main industry. The banks, the universities, the cafes, the souvenir shops which sold the nearly authentic relics: they all thrived on God. Survived by creating a city devoted to devotion.

In Tournai, God, apparently, was as common as air.

The baker said he saw Him in a cherry tart. The milliner, in the eye of a peacock feather. The trash man said he saw Him tumbling down the alleyways in the white grease of the *frietzaks*, the abandoned paper cones, their twice-fried potatoes eaten long ago. These sightings of God were well documented in newspapers and radio broadcasts. They were proudly spoken of in the streets.

"Did you know that the barber saw the face of the Virgin on the floor of his shop yesterday?"

"No, but I heard the butcher found a small cross within the belly of a lamb."

Everywhere, everyone saw God. How could they not? In Tournai, seeing God was a matter of civic pride.

Then bombs came. Then soldiers. Then silence.

Now recruitment posters cover the church doors. *Ersatz kommando der waffen!* The Germans are asking for help. Support us! they say, and show the enemy in his "true light"—a red devil, the Star of David around his neck. The devil laughs at the cross, crushes Belgium with his pitchfork.

Some of the priests, their churches in rubble, ask their congregations to consider the Germans' position. Did not the Jews betray our Savior? they ask.

Ersatz kommando der waffen!

Since the occupation began, it is said that God has not been seen in Tournai. It is believed that He quietly slipped away. Heartbroken, He eased himself out of the situation, unsure if He would ever return.

2

She used to think they had horns of white chocolate. Or, so it was said. Wrapped in sharp linen, two pure chocolate horns growing out of their heads.

One can understand the mistake. Marie Claire was just a child. They were Belgian nuns. Though the finest chocolate in the world is from Belgium, no one in Marie Claire's village has seen chocolate for a long time. Everywhere she looks— the snow, the heavy stars, the stone streets where she is given the slice of bread that she and her grandmother, Paulette, will eat for three days—are all made of chocolate.

Even the soldiers, their tin eyes, must be chocolate.

These are the details: March, 1941, France. A small village

on the Belgian border, near Tournai. The village's name is not remembered.

What is remembered has neither time nor place.

Marie Claire and Paulette are in the greenhouse, near the center of the village. It's their family business, or what's left of it. Last week another riot took nearly all the windows. On the few that remain, the word "Jude" was painted. The ragged yellow letters overlap, keep the sun from tender shoots. When she can, Paulette covers the seedlings with glass jars she finds in the streets. Tells herself it's temporary. Makes plans to rebuild.

In the corner of the greenhouse are the irises, arranged by color in long, tall rows. Each row is a slightly different shade of blue—from the brush of smoke to the deep, deep blue of a starless night. It is a dark horizon. Marie Claire imagines her grandmother has planted the heavens for her. But today, not even the heavens are safe.

No time left, her grandmother says, no time at all. Her grandmother's long silver hair swings back and forth like sheets of rain. She pushes it away from her face with a trembling hand. "The irises are quite delicate," she tells Marie Claire and shows her grandchild how to wrap the flowers gently. "Wet the fabric first," she says, and hands the small girl a bit of cloth. "Now, twist it around the roots." The iris bulbs are fat as shallots but their roots are frail. "You must always protect the roots," Paulette says. Wraps a bulb deftly. Reaches for the next.

The irises are to be Marie Claire's legacy, that's what Paulette has told her. Her grandmother named them after her, "Marie Claire." They took seven years to grow—just as she took seven years. Petals as black as her own hair. Big as a man's fist. Her grandmother told her they were very special. Nobody had ever grown a black iris before.

Marie Claire knows her grandmother wants her to be very careful, but she lets the bulb slide from her hand. To her, the roots look like small fingers, reaching.

"You'll hurt them," Paulette scolds, then regrets the tone of her voice.

Marie Claire's eyes fill with tears, she didn't mean to hurt them. Their baby fingers.

"Try again," Paulette says, kisses the top of Marie Claire's head. "Try again, my darling."

Marie Claire nods. Picks up another bulb. Her hair is loosely braided into two black ropes, badly looped and fraying, tossed over her shoulders like reins with no rider. She is small for her age and stands on her toes to reach the workbench. Her arms are crooked as kindling. When she leans forward to shake dirt from around a bulb, the backs of her shoes remain on the floor. The humus, its thick, damp smell, makes her eyes water. Marie Claire's dress is quickly turning from sky blue to black, coated with mud, water, and her own sweat. Her skin is cold, plucked like a hen.

"That's better," Paulette says, watching Marie Claire carefully wrap the fat bulbs.

Today is Tuesday. Out of habit, Paulette is wearing her best dress, the one with the small red roses. The black background flatters Paulette's slim waist, the elegant pale of her skin, her blue eyes clear as desire. Every Tuesday Paulette wears this dress. It is Marie Claire's favorite. The child imagines that each rose is real and fragrant as summer. Hundreds and hundreds of roses. The smell is so sweet, Marie Claire can hardly breathe.

The Durrieu Family Greenhouse was once very well known for its rose hybrids. Her grandmother bred roses so dark and so heavy with fragrance that fashionable women floated the dried petals in their baths. Marie Claire still remembers what those roses smelled like. They smelled like Tuesday, the best day of all. The day of Monsieur Boubais' weekly visit.

Before the war, M. Boubais was a famous man, a mask maker from Binche. He came to France out of love for a widow whom he had met on a train. He didn't know Paulette was a Jew. When she told him he turned away. It was just a reflex, he said, like a sneeze. I love you, he said. She turned away. Even though he did love her, she couldn't believe him.

So, every Tuesday for nearly a year, M. Boubais asked Paulette to become his wife. Then the soldiers came and they would not let him leave—even if he wanted to, which he did not. Jew-lover, they said. Yes, he would reply, even though it was not a question. More than anything in the world, he wanted Paulette to be his wife, for her and Marie Claire to become his family.

A jolly, jolly family.

Today, her grandmother has told Marie Claire that there is no time for such things. "Love has become impossible," Paulette says, mostly to herself.

One by one, Marie Claire and her grandmother take the irises gently from the clay pots. The child wraps the bulbs in damp strips torn from the blankets of her bed. "I am sorry," she whispers to each bulb. They do not fall away from the dirt easily. Marie Claire imagines the ground as a warm, safe home. "I am very sorry," she says so quietly her words barely move through the tight air.

Outside the ragged glass walls, the soldiers seem to have left. The air feels like a breath inhaled. "It is too quiet," her grandmother says. Marie Claire is confused. When she saw the trains arrive from her bedroom window, she thought it was good news. She was happy as she jumped up and down on her grandmother's bed. Very happy.

"The world is not that simple," her grandmother said, and told Marie Claire to get dressed, and to hurry. Marie Claire watched in silence as her grandmother ran up and down the street, shouting, waking the neighbors. So much confusion and then to the greenhouse to wake the irises, her irises.

The child shakes another iris from its soil. The blue-black petals tremble so slightly. The bulb is muddy. Marie Claire doesn't care, she holds it close to her heart with tenderness. Paulette watches her for a moment, "It is good to be careful," she says. Marie Claire understands. Her parents were not careful. Marie Claire misses them very much.

Shh. Shh. She says to herself whenever she thinks of them. *Shh.* They were shot standing in a fountain so everyone could watch their blood flow over and over again. A soldier held Marie Claire by the arm. She didn't know his name. Her hand went numb. Everyone had to watch. Even grandmother.

Shh.

Today the trains have arrived and Marie Claire is confused. Everyone should be happy, she thinks. Now that the trains are here, she and Grandmama will be taken to the farms where they will plant raspberries for tarts and strawberries for jam. And roses, hundreds and hundreds of roses. That's what the soldiers said. No one will be hungry again.

Everyone should be happy.

But now, outside the damp glass of the greenhouse, Marie Claire can see that everyone is leaving.

Everyone who can is leaving.

The butcher drags his three-legged goat. A mother with her baby in one arm, like a sack of flour, runs wild, barefoot, back and forth down the stone street. Ankles twist. She is screaming, Which way? Which way? Marie Claire cannot watch. The woman nearly topples the Hebrew teacher on his solemn black bicycle. He swerves. His long beard trails behind him like a tail on a kite.

"It is better to die in Paris," he shouts to her, "Follow me!"

The woman begins to run behind him. Her baby, bouncing, is red-faced, gasping. Marie Claire is afraid.

When the last of the irises are gathered, Paulette picks up her black leather book. Marie Claire's small hand runs along the book's cracked spine. Its brittle pages.

"Yes, can't forget this," Paulette says, and carefully wraps the frail notebook in the last strip of sheet. "Without my notes, the work is useless." Paulette gently places the notebook in her cutting basket, layers the wrapped bulbs on top of the book, until the basket is overflowing. "Now," she says, but before she can say anything else, the air hisses.

The irises, their bruised eyes, turn away.

"Run," Paulette screams, grabs the basket, pushes Marie Claire out of the greenhouse. What remains of the glass door shatters behind them.

Outside, all around, others are running. Like so many ants. The hiss of air explodes. They're thrown like dice. Marie Claire. Her grandmother. The irises, like crows, like Marie Claire, take flight. The sky rumbles, pitches, and heaves, fitful as sleep.

Then silence, like a slap.

The sleep of shock is immeasurable.

When Marie Claire finally wakes, her head is a tunnel without light. The surprise of bricks and bodies carelessly tossed upon the street makes her laugh for no reason. When she finally remembers the sound of her own voice, "They are like wax dolls," she says, pushing the bodies off of her small, thin frame. They do not move easily. The bodies rock back and forth, lazy with weight.

She cannot find her grandmother in this tangle—the hands, the feet, the ice of glass—so she runs, runs away, runs from these dolls, their wax eyes, their familiar smell. She runs fast as the moment will carry her, past the bakery, past the post office, past all that once stood, now reduced to a memory of stone and gravel.

She can't stop laughing.

Marie Claire turns the corner to her street. *Yes*. Her grandmother's house is still standing. Its hip roof. The half-moon shutters. A beacon. Marie Claire can see it. It propels her forward. She knows her grandmother will be there.

Wait.

As the child nears, she can see something. A dark lump of something blocking the door.

Closer. Careful.

Like a small mountain.

Oh.

This something, this dark lump is M. Boubais. *Beloved*. The mask maker from Binche who used his jolly face for a model. "It appeals to my vanity," he once told Marie Claire, and winked. He was the kind of man who liked to wink.

Now Marie Claire stands over him. Winks. She doesn't know what else to do. He looks like a harlequin, she thinks to herself, and laughs again. It's only natural. He does. Half his face is burned black.

Love has become impossible, her grandmother said, but Marie Claire can still feel it, scratching.

Stop laughing.

The man is a mountain to the small child. Solid. Round. In the street, Marie Claire hears the soldiers. She cannot stop laughing. The rumble of their German. The laughing hurts her sides. She cannot catch her breath. The soldiers are firing rounds and rounds into the air: at dogs, at the wind itself, at anything that moves or catches their eye. Marie Claire wants to stop laughing but cannot. She hears a voice.

"Jump."

Marie Claire turns, there is no one there. She moves closer to the door. "Who is speaking?" she says. No answer. There is no one, nothing, except the smell of roses.

"Jump."

This time the word is loud. A command. An order. Marie Claire notices that the door to her grandmother's kitchen opens, just a bit, as if someone wants her to enter. The voice is coming from inside.

"Jump."

The child jumps. Her foot drags slightly, catching the cleft of M. Boubais' chin. She turns. His vacant face. Stray eye. The mouth goes slack. Marie Claire has stopped laughing. She slams the kitchen door. The house is dark. She blinks.

"Grandmama?"

No one responds. The kitchen is empty. The house, uneasy with the warp of its own timber, is silent. Outside, Marie

Claire can hear soldiers. Gunfire. A laugh. More shouting. The creak of the warped step, second from the top. *Someone is standing on the porch.* Kicking. Kicking something. Hard.

M. Boubais, she thinks, and covers her ears. The brass doorknob jiggles. Her sweat rolls onto the dust of the kitchen floor. Someone shouts in German. A palm slaps the door. Hard. Kicking. *They are kicking the door.*

Marie Claire falls to her knees. The root cellar, she thinks, and pulls back the rug next to the stove. Her grandmother told her she would be safe in the root cellar.

She pulls the door. Hard. Too hard. It swings open, wide, throws Marie Claire off balance. She hits the dirt of the cellar floor. The room telescopes, a pure and blinding light. Above her, for just a moment, she sees what she thinks is a hand, somehow familiar. Small red roses encircle a gentle wrist. The cellar door slams.

The world is in her throat.

Shafts of light cross the basement floor, thin as razors. There is a sound, like a rug being dragged across the kitchen floor. The kitchen door splinters.

nonono . . .

They are inside.

Above is the sound of so many boots, pounding the uneven floorboards.

Dirt falls through the cracks.

Marie Claire is caught in a shower of splinters and dirt. It covers her face, her eyes. Above her, the sound of chairs breaking.

She cannot scream.

Her mouth is open but she cannot scream.

She pulls the dirt around her, taking fistfuls from the cellar floor, until she is covered, invisible in her own mind. She feels herself take root.

Soon, everything is silent.

Soon, silence is all that remains.

Grandmama, M. Boubais, the irises—big as a man's fist— all fade from the fabric of Marie Claire's memory. This is not a sad thing. In the dark safety of the root cellar, the world is so sweet. The air is cool, cool, calm as earth. This place once breathed of potatoes, of parsnips and turnips: all silent, all roots pulled from the ground. The onions peeled away, gently, like the hours, layer by layer.

Curled in the darkness, Marie Claire feels cool and safe in the dirt. She is planted in this place. It is her home.

3

WINK. WINK.

"Are you ready, Marie Claire?" The voice of M. Boubais fills her head, like a thought, but he is nowhere to be seen.

Shh, the child thinks but cannot say. Above her, her grandmother's house grows cold. The timber dries, hollows itself. Marie Claire's body, too, hollows itself. The bones dry. The blood flakes within the veins.

No matter. Dust will always return to dust.

Marie Claire is sitting in what she imagines to be a greenhouse, a small glass house as humid as tears. It is not her family's greenhouse, but a greenhouse nonetheless. The thunderclouds of irises, their tired eyes. Thousands of windowpanes streaked with burnished light.

And everywhere there are stars.

Scattered on the floor like cobblestones, their old, golden light warms Marie Claire's feet. They hang from the ceiling on odd bits of string, lazy in their brilliance. Even the chair upon which she sits is soft with light, and creaks. Marie Claire has never sat on stars before. They are warmer than she imagined. Soft as something forgotten.

Marie Claire is sitting in front of a puppet theater made from old boxes held together with bits of string. Hurly burly. The theater is perched at an odd angle, leans this way and that. It is large, large enough for her to stand in, stretch her fingers from side to side, but she does not move. The promise of seeing M. Boubais again keeps her firmly in her seat.

Are you ready, my dear? His voice booms. Marie Claire's head vibrates with the sound. Why are you hiding? she thinks. She knows she should be afraid but the show is about to begin.

Klezmer music roars to life like elephants leaping on cymbals; a swift river of bells; accordions with chainsaw riffs and fire-breathing fiddles. The current of music eddies, bounces, and shakes. Marie Claire is uneasy with pleasure. The puppet theater leans to one side, and then to the next, as if keeping time to the cyclone of sound, faster and faster and tight as a fist.

"Welcome!"

M. Boubais steps from behind the stage. Grandly. A flourish. Bows. His face sags like wax, still melting, but jolly.

His striped shirt is at odds with his small round of flesh. It is stretched to the limit around him, makes him seem as round as a beet.

"Let the show begin!" he says. Winks. Claps wildly. Hoots and cheers for himself. Marie Claire is silent. Tries to wink.

The light of the stars dims.

Shh.

Show time.

The music is a whirlwind. M. Boubais, the famous mask maker as puppeteer, takes his place behind the cardboard theater. It tilts, lurches forward. He cannot fit behind it. His belly is overripe. He laughs. This awkward universe shakes.

The music sparks, jolly jolly.

The curtain opens, the music shimmers. It takes Marie Claire a moment to adjust to the darkness. Her eyes widen like a cat's. Shapes come into focus, slowly. She can see that there is something in the center of the stage, a pile of some sort, but the stage is so dark, it's difficult to see what exactly is in the pile. She squints.

What is this? she thinks.

M. Boubais leans out from behind the stage. "The future," he says, and strikes a match, casually tosses it onto the pile. Jumps back behind the stage.

The flame immediately takes root, engulfs the pile, illuminates it. It appears to be a mountain of things, ordinary things: dresses, shoes, books, suitcases, a doll. The fire cradles it all within a single flame that tapers to a point, like the head of a match. Marie Claire wants to run, but still cannot move. Tears fall from her eyes involuntarily. She cannot wipe them away.

Flames shoot higher and higher, lick the top of the rickety theater. Marie Claire knows that at any moment its toothless walls will go up in flames, taking everything in the greenhouse with them: her, the irises, M. Boubais. In the light of the blazing fire, she can make out all manner of things that are burning. Women's shoes, thick-heeled. A small cloth bear, whose glass eyes fall to the floor like dice.

Marie Claire wants to ask whose things these are—is there anything that belongs to her, or grandmother—but speech is impossible.

M. Boubais leans out from behind the burning stage. "Look," he says and points to the bonfire. Then jumps back behind the stage again, so merry, as if he were a child again playing hide-and-seek.

Marie Claire looks closely at the stage. In the cool blue center of the fire a hand appears, a woman's hand wearing a simple gold band. It reaches out to Marie Claire, nearly touching her.

She wants to scream but cannot.

"Take it," M. Boubais says from somewhere inside of her.

Marie Claire shakes her head.

"Take it. Go on." The words hiss from one ear to another. From where she sits, Marie Claire can see the fire burning away at the flesh of the hand, peeling it back like a plum. Muscle falls from the bone.

"You have to take it."

"Where are you?" she screams, the words finally escaping.

Fire leaps onto the curtain, which torches the stage. Stars begin to melt, drip by drip, fold into themselves, around the small girl. So warm, they coat her flesh, fill each pore: her feet, her ankles, the soft of her knees. Within seconds, the floor is a shining sea around her. Marie Claire is bobbing, gasping for breath. There is no horizon, no sky. Within the flames M. Boubais is floating, afire, like a cruise liner, melting into the color of irises, spreading, skimming across this rapid, dark ocean.

"There is no need to be afraid ever again," M. Boubais says from everywhere and nowhere at once.

"Take the hand when it is offered and you will be with us all again. A jolly, jolly family."

4

MANY DAYS PASS BEFORE THE CELLAR DOOR OPENS
and they stand above her: Anne, the postulate, and the Reverend Mother Superior Sister Xavier.

Peering.

The Sisters of His Divine and Most Sacred Blood of Tournai. Their motto: The World Needs Brave and Joyful Women of Faith. Their headdress: horns of white chocolate. Their habits: a dusty cocoa. This rescue mission is not their first. They have come to save the children, they say. You are safe, they say. You are lucky.

No one else in the village has survived.

Outside the kitchen door, on the back stairs, the body of a man—once fat, once jolly, a man who liked to wink—is half-eaten away by crows, and the industry of ants. His striped shirt waves in the wind. The smell of rotting flesh makes the nuns' eyes water.

The Reverend Mother Xavier leans in closer to the child. Her lamp is bright. The child blinks. Mother Xavier, like the child, is a survivor. Before the war, the Sisters of His Divine and Most Sacred Blood were nearly thirty in number.

Now, even the sound of breath has weight.

Some fled. Some were unlucky. Some were overcome by age. Last week, only three remained. Today, only two.

There is a dark hand, like a cloud, covering Mother Xavier's heart. The one who died she had loved most of all. She and Sister Ruth were childhood friends. They wore each other's histories like coats, rolled-up sleeves, fraying hems.

The Reverend Mother's silver cross floats above Marie Claire, catches the light. Jesus smiles, so weary. "Take my hand," she says, and leans into the cellar with the agility of a dancer. Her face is deeply lined from the sun, the ascetic life of the convent. Her hand trembles, uneasy.

Take the hand when offered. Marie Claire hears M. Boubais' voice, but can see that the hand has no ring. I am safe here, she thinks. *Safe.*

Anne, the postulate, holds Mother Xavier's other hand with both of hers. She balances the nun as best she can but her feet are unsteady. Wave after wave of nausea makes her hands sweat. An eddy of red hair slips from beneath her veil. Another curl slips out. An unruly storm.

Marie Claire coughs. Mother Xavier smiles, warmly, trying

to please. "Soon as I saw the rug," she says to Marie Claire, "I knew there was something underneath it. Who puts a rug next to a stove?"

Mother Xavier shakes her fingers as if they are wet. "Come on," she says, her voice too gay, forced. "Take my hand. I can't pull you up without your help."

Marie Claire shuts her eyes, as if to go to sleep, to dream the cellar door closed, to dream these odd women away.

"Is she hurt, Reverend Mother?" Anne whispers. "She seems to be buried." The acid of her stomach rises up to her throat. Burns.

Mother Xavier peers over the steel rim of her glasses. "She's up to her neck," she says, suddenly tired, the adrenaline gone.

"What should we do?" Anne asks. The cool sun beats through the windows. Stratas of stench make the air feel thick. She bites her lower lip, so as not to vomit. I don't want to make matters worse, she thinks.

Slowly, the Reverend Mother tries to stand up straight. A dull pain spreads across her lower back, makes her see the world at a tilt. I am too old for this, she thinks, although she is not old. Her heart is bad, her breath often short. She is shaking her head and mumbling, "I don't know, I don't know." She looks around the splintered kitchen. Shards of glass cover the floor. Outside, the body. "Perhaps we're too late for her, too."

Anne takes a deep breath, *steady*, peers into the cellar, at the child. Her face is gray. *Can't let her die.*

"Let us pray for guidance," Mother Xavier says, crosses herself as if to pray but can only think of Sister Ruth, her lifeless body floating downriver and the Commander's flint eyes. Mother Xavier's fingers work the rosary's wooden beads, unvarnished, dark with the oil from her own flesh. *Ruth, beloved. Ruth, the blessed.*

Anne bows her head in prayer. Sweat pours down her face. *The child is dying. The child is dying.*

Mother Xavier sinks to the stone floor in a litany of prayer. *Ruth the fair. Ruth the kind.*

The lack of sleep and food, the sickly sharp smell of death. "Maybe if we went outside," Anne says, slowly chewing the words as she speaks them, quickly being overcome by the moment, losing her sense of language and self. "Maybe if we went outside and got some air."

Mother Xavier doesn't seem to hear. Her head is in her hands.

Anne prays *Hear us, O Lord, Almighty Father, eternal God and deign to send thy holy angel from heaven to show the way* but wants, desperately, to leave this place. No holy angel. No divine intervention. All she wants is to go back to the convent and take a hot bath. Breathe clear air.

She and Mother Xavier have been looking for survivors for nearly a week. *So long, too long, without much sleep.* The wool of her habit has rubbed her skin raw. Just an hour ago, she discovered a flea burrowing its way underneath the cuff of her sleeve. This will be simple, Mother Xavier said. Just slip across the border and home again. Anne knew she was right. It should have been simple, they'd done it many times before. But this time the circumstances were different.

So much destruction.

Still on her knees, Anne leans into the basement. The child's mouth is open, cracked as tar. Still breathing, Anne thinks, and reaches into the dark cellar toward the child. She hears a fluttering of wings.

Bats.

Anne wants to pull away. Her heart beats faster. Her hands sweat. She bites her lower lip hard. They won't hurt me, she thinks.

Holy Mother of God, pray for us sinners now and at the hour of our death.

She takes a deep breath. *They won't hurt me.*

"Wake up," she says. The child does not move. Anne reaches in farther, as far as she can go. *Close.* So close she can feel the child's shallow breath brush her fingertips. Just then, something flies past her face. Anne screams, jerks backward.

Coward.

Anne is shaking uncontrollably. The feeling of utter use-lessness overwhelms her.

Miserable coward.

I am sorry, Anne says to Marie Claire and then to Mother Xavier and then to God. Anne is often sorry, very sorry: sorry for things beyond her control; sorry for every breath she takes.

Right now, in her pocket, chocolates melt, despite the

chill of a restless spring. A handful, enough for an entire village in times such as these, but nearly taken for granted by Anne. They are part of the fabric of her life. Anne's father owns several shops throughout Belgium, two in Brussels alone, and a factory near his home, near the convent, in Tournai. M. Remy Mathot is rich, very rich, with Anne as an only child, not the son he needed to carry on the family business.

A disappointing daughter, a lumbering girl.

That is how Anne sees herself. When she prays to God, she sees His face as her father's face. The waves of silver hair. Remy's ivory skin. Forgive me, Father, she begins, imagines Remy, the last time she saw him. The hunch of his shoulders as he turned away from her. The shaking of his hands. The taste of blood in her mouth. Nearly a year has passed since she's seen him.

Only say the word and I shall be healed.

Every week a box of chocolates arrives at the convent. Anne never sees it delivered. It is slid between the bars of the iron gates. On the top of the pink cardboard box is the family seal—"Remy Mathot and Sons."

Sons.

Anne hardly notices the word anymore.

I am unworthy, but speak the word and I shall be healed.

Hardly notices it at all.

At first, the chocolates were perfect. Beautiful, dark. Inside a ripe fruit: a tiny wild raspberry or tight-lipped currant. On the top of each chocolate, a small golden "M," for Mathot, crafted from spun sugar.

But now, well.

Haphazard. Some without centers. A caramel gone too soft. The slight taste of bitterness on the tongue. Imperfect, but it doesn't matter. Anne doesn't mind. The chocolates, whatever state they arrive in, are a sign that despite the war the factory has reopened and she is still remembered. They are a sign that all is well, as well as can be expected.

She eats them greedily, sometimes by the handful.

Marie Claire turns her head slightly. An onionskin cough. Anne's heart cannot bear it. Marie Claire coughs again, weaker this time. A rasp of breath.

Without thinking, Anne reaches down to her again.

We will wash you, wrap you in warm blankets. We will take you where it's safe.

The child's eyes open, as if she has heard what has not been said. Anne reaches into her pocket.

"Look, chocolate," Anne says, and offers it with dull hands.

The sound of beating wings grows louder.

The child looks at Anne, wanting.

They can't hurt me, Anne thinks, and focuses only on the child, not the dark, not what could be in the dark. *She cannot die.* Marie Claire is the most beautiful creature Anne has ever seen. The luminescence of her skin, the blue black of her hair, and the smell of roses, fat and fragrant, overwhelm Anne. She begins to cry huge, hapless tears.

Marie Claire's mouth opens but she does not speak. She does not move. Anne's tears are a gentle rain which fills the child's throat, a warm river fragrant with salt. Time softens around them. Marie Claire's breath is labored with new life. Stumbling. In her veins, the blood grows warm again. She lifts her hand to Anne, to the chocolate. Rose petals fall from her dirt-caked dress. Her lips move. A word. Anne leans closer. Marie Claire's breath is cold as memory.

"Jump," Marie Claire says softly.

The sound of beating wings surrounds them. They're everywhere, Anne thinks, panics, and yanks the child into her arms. Chocolates tumble onto the cellar floor.

"You are safe now," Anne says. Kisses Marie Claire on her forehead.

Out of the darkness of the cellar, a cold wind. Something pushes past them, at least it feels like something, but nothing is there. *Imagining things.*

She looks into the cellar. The chocolates are gone.

"You are safe," she says again. *I am just imagining things.*

Later, when Mother Xavier speaks of the rescue of Marie Claire, she will say it was the chocolate that saved her. Lured her.

"Anne's horns of white chocolate," she will say, laugh, uneasy, and pour herself another cognac.

But when the miracles begin, the Reverend Mother stops laughing.

5

THE COMMANDER STANDS BEHIND THE CONVENT of the Sisters of His Divine and Most Sacred Blood of Tournai. Alone. The river bends here, shoots down the round of the hill. Wild rapids. Deadly. He stands on a thin ledge of the bank. Investigating.

A few days ago, just a bit downstream, he shot what seemed to be a man loading a family of Jews on a raft. The Jews ran into the night. The man, dressed in black pants, dark sweater, took the shot in the chest, fell back onto the makeshift boat, then down through the rapids.

In the moonlight, as the man fell, the Commander caught a glimpse of what he thought was a woman's face. The softness of its line. It was a face he knew he had seen somewhere before but could not place. A face like those renderings of

Saint Martha. Martha, the sister of Lazarus. Martha, the self-less, the one who served all who had needs without question.

Martha the Holy, the Pure.

It was Martha's face and yet, a traitor's.

With great difficulty, the Commander retraces what he believes was the Jews' path. It leads him here to the narrow ledge, along the river behind the convent. *A nun's face.*

All along the slope of the river's edge, trees and undergrowth warp and weave. Catch his legs. Scratch his shoes.

The Commander had been told by Father Pascal, the parish priest, that at one time the river was not as large as it is today. Fifty years ago a dam broke upstream, flooded the banks. A summer of torrential rains made it worse. Now, trees grow where houses once stood. Only the convent remains. Hangs on the edge of a hill.

At least for now.

On clear days, its high stone walls are reflected in the river like a mirror, but darker.

A perfect base for the Resistance.

As a Catholic, the Commander finds the idea incomprehensible. *Are we not on the same side?* As a soldier, he understands that the Belgians will surrender in body only, knows that in Tournai there is a seething, barely perceptible. For his men, limited in number and stationed in a town that is not strategically important, the river is a tactical problem. For the Resistance, with their American guns and handmade rafts, the river is an opportunity for subversion. For Jews, on moonless nights, it is a river of freedom, sometimes a river of death, but there is no choice, no choice at all.

Much can be hidden in this river and much is. The sisters, the Commander suspects, know that very well. Their fortressed walls. Their downturned eyes. They are a community of nuns that is spoken of as eccentric, unworldly. Pious beyond reproach. The Reverend Mother Xavier herself is German, her own parents work for the Reich. The Commander delivers their letters on a weekly basis. Who'd suspect her? he thinks, satisfied that he does.

The Commander removes his cap by its brim and adjusts the peak. This was not the life he wanted, but he believes he has adapted well. Nearly thirty, the wheat of his hair is thinning, patches of pink scalp shine through the crosshatch on his crown. A blueness to his eyes suggests the sky of pilots: sheer air, unexpected danger.

The Commander is very careful about his uniform. He's sewn a knife pleat into his pants so they will never looked wrinkled. He has also sewn the pockets closed so he will not forget and place his hands inside of them. *Untidy.*

The space of grass on which he stands is not large enough for a man of his size but he stands there anyway. It provides him a clear view of the river, its relationship to the convent. He squints, thinks he sees something near the center of the stone wall. A dark square, not more than three feet wide and three feet high. *A chute of some sort, perhaps for coal.* It's just a few feet away but he can't reach it. *The ledge narrows there, even more*. He knows the water below him is deep. *A man could drown. But a nun as small and wiry as Mother Xavier would have no problem walking that ledge.*

Carefully, he shifts his weight to his toes to get a better view. *It definitely looks like a coal chute.* It appears to be propped open, as if recently used. Water from the river's edge laps over the toes of his shoes, threatens his socks.

The Commander feels the bank shift beneath him. Dirt, which supported his weight only a moment ago, falls into the water. He places his hand along the wall to steady himself. Tiny bits of stone cut his long fingers, the fat of his palm, draw lines of blood. The blood rises, defines his hand as if he suddenly has two life lines, and in a sense, he does.

He has been here before, on this hill, in better times. *Nearly a year ago to the date.* He wishes it were not so. Even now, the scent of Shalimar haunts him. Even now, his heart speeds, without meter, at the sight of this river where he and Anne ate small sweet strawberries that were the color of her hair in the heat of day. *Anne.* Her awkward beauty. The unruly waves of hair. The grass giving way beneath them. The soft smell of green, the same color as her eyes.

If she were dead, I would know it. The uncertainty distracts him.

Before the Germans took Belgium, the Commander was a member of an intelligence squad; his specialty was cartography. He entered several cities, such as Tournai, and set about mapping their weaknesses. Bridges that were crucial. Canals that could force a gridlock. With charcoals and paper, he posed as a student, sketching the wonders of Belgium. Its most populated cathedrals, Ground Zero.

He had always been the enemy.

After the city surrendered, nearly a year ago, he was stationed in Tournai assigned the rank of Commander. A logical choice, they told him. You know the lay of the land, quite well, they said. And the people too.

It is very difficult to keep secrets from the Reich.

But even though he knew he was being watched, when the Commander arrived in Tournai he went directly to Anne's father's factory. The gold-lettered sign creaked as it rocked back and forth: Mathot & Sons, Chocolatier. The factory was closed, wood covered the office windows, but the Commander tried the door. It opened without a sound.

In the reception area, a dusty light filtered through the cracks in the boards that covered the windows. The air smelled of chocolate, dense and nearly unbreathable. As his eyes adjusted to the grayness, the Commander could see that the room was simply furnished with three leather chairs arranged around a low, elaborately carved table. Probably rosewood, he thought. It was too dark to tell for sure. On the table was what appeared to be an ornate silver tray with a dozen or more truffles on white paper lace.

It had been a long time since the Commander had eaten

Belgian chocolates, or any kind of chocolate for that matter. Even in the dim light, they were beautiful, some dusted in powdered sugar, some topped with cocoa beans.

The Commander's stomach began to growl, low. The pureness of wanting took hold. He felt like a child again. Looked over his shoulder. No one seemed to be in the room.

Just one.

Quickly, the Commander picked a truffle off the tray, the one nearest him. It was fat and round, dark chocolate marbled with light. He lifted it to his mouth, salivating, imagining its warm sweetness, how it melts on the tongue, but before he could bite, he felt something. An odd something. Something in his hand. Crawling.

In the half-light of the room, he examined the chocolate closely. It was only a shell. The interior had been eaten away from underneath. *Ants.* The truffle was filled with dozens and dozens of ants, their curious heads, shiny and hungry, crawling onto his palm, falling onto his lips, rolling down his sleeve.

He threw the truffle down and begin to spit. *What was I thinking? What was I thinking?* The table, which he mistook for being carved, was covered with ants. Red and black, their bodies moving back and forth, undulating armies, twisting around the table legs, the silver tray, the small cocoa beans, even the white paper, which their bodies had turned into lace. He could feel them crawling down his throat.

He wiped his mouth frantically with his sleeve, wiped until his eyes watered, the dry skin of his lips peeled away. When the frenzy was over, *Like an animal*, he thought, disgusted. *This is what I have come to.*

As he looked around the room, he could see that the ants were everywhere, climbing the leather chairs, the wallpaper, the thick carpet that moved beneath his feet. He wanted to run, but curiosity took hold.

How long has this place been vacant?

He crossed to the secretary's desk. With a quick hand, he brushed aside the ants from the appointment book that lay open. *May 14, 1940*. The day before the bombing. *A week. One week.*

He picked up an ant that was crawling on his cheek and looked at it closely. The head moved this way and that. The mouth was open, eating air, waiting for something better to cross its path. Only a week had passed and already the ants appeared to have taken over the factory, bit by bit. They needed no tanks, the Commander thought. *No bombs. No planes. No Commanders.*

Behind the secretary's desk was a door with the name "M. Remy Mathot, Proprietor" gold-lettered in a baroque script. For no particular reason, the Commander opened the door. Remy was seated at his desk, his hands folded in front of him, as if waiting for another card to be dealt.

Daylight, slanting through the boarded windows, outlined

the old man's quivering body. For a moment, the Commander wasn't sure if Remy was awake, or even alive.

"Monsieur Mathot?"

The Commander turned on the desk lamp. The old man blinked. The ants scurried from his hands, his arms.

"Are you all right?"

"I know you," he said.

"Yes," the Commander nodded. "I'm here to see Anne." He held his hat in hand, a suitor.

"I see," Remy said, but said no more. It was noon. Outside, in the street, what remained of the bells of Tournai began to ring, chime, peal the hour. Four hundred bells, now only a dozen or more. The sound of their calling seemed distant as youth.

Remy's mouth opened slightly as if to speak, but he couldn't find the words. Despite the faintness of the music, his body shook, his bones vibrated with the bells, bells that refused to be silent, refused to give in to the destruction that surrounded them.

For Remy, each bell that remains, every hour, calls her name.

Minouche. Me-noo-sh. Mee-nooo-shh. Meee-noo-sh.

Minouche, his wife. Last week, after the first air strike, Remy found her body in the rubble of St. Mark's Cathedral. She had insisted on going to church alone. The week before she had been released from a private hospital. More than a decade there. Religious delusion, her chart read. Every day they ran electricity through her body. Every day at 9 a.m., sharp. Her doctor joked, told Remy it was her wake-up call.

The idea of Minouche returning to the church never occurred to him. She could see it on his face.

I'm fine, she said. If I weren't, they wouldn't have let me come home.

But I've missed you.

And I've missed God.

What could you have done? Anne had said to him, weeping in the rubble of St. Mark's, wiping the blood from her mother's face.

Remy didn't seem to hear. *The cream of her skin. Her burnished hair.* He pushed Anne away gently. Took Minouche into his arms.

Meee-noo-sh.

Minouche's skin was still warm as he held her. As he kissed her he could taste the blush of her lips, still sweet. Anne turned away. Held her breath.

Let's go home now, he said to Minouche.

Anne was silent as he carried her mother's body home, then into their bedroom. We need to sleep, he said to Anne. We are very tired. Then Remy closed the door and lay with Minouche in their bed. Naked. Flesh to flesh.

Day to night for three days, he slept heavy and unmoving, dreaming of endless fog and nothing more. He didn't notice when the bedroom door finally opened, when Anne gently lifted her mother's body from his arms.

Just seven days had passed since the first bomb; since Minouche's death; since Belgium surrendered. Since the occupation began. Just seven days, but so much had changed. Seven days ago, Remy wore his success like a well-tailored suit, but at this moment, the old man was broken, unshaven, wearing clothes he'd slept in for days.

In the street, the bells of St. Luke's began the *Ode to Joy*. It took six strong men to perform it properly. Now with only boys available, young boys, and their grandmothers, the tune wandered unsure and confused.

"Are you all right?" the Commander asked Remy again, not knowing what else to say. The young man shifted his weight from foot to foot. Like a wave, the sheen of his black leather shoes rippled in the light of the desk lamp. I mean no harm, he wanted to say, but knew that statement had no basis in truth. I am the enemy, he thought, and the words surprised him, as if he had somehow forgotten.

"I'm hoping Anne will see me," the Commander said. "I need to know if you would permit that."

Outside the bells faltered, then stopped ringing mid-refrain. Unfinished, it continued on in Remy's head. He looked at the Commander, red-eyed like a spider, covered his ears with his hands. "It's the silence I can't bear," he said. A vein of ants crawled up his sleeve.

The Commander ran his fingers along the visor of his cap.

Looked down as he spoke. "I assure you," he said, feeling a sudden shyness, a need for approval, "that I am most sincere in my affections."

The words pushed Remy out of his grief, into the moment. In his mind, bits and pieces of logic surfaced. *He loves her. He'll take her from me.* I should kill him, he thought.

"Anne is dead," he said.

For a moment, the Commander wasn't sure if he heard the old man right.

"Killed with her mother at the church," Remy said quickly. His eyes shifting from place to place. Before the Commander could inquire any further, the old man stood.

"If you'll excuse me," Remy said. Shaking. Watching the gun. The proximity to the Commander's hand. *I could kill him if I tried. I know I could.*

The Commander was unsure if he should believe the old man. This was not the Remy he knew. Not the confident man so willing to marry his daughter to an artist who professed rich parents. But still, his demeanor spoke of great loss, the dementia that follows.

"I'm sorry," the Commander said, mostly to himself, and gently closed the office door behind him. *I will always be the enemy.* He knew it didn't matter if the old man was lying. Anne would never be his. He vomited in the secretary's wastebasket.

When the Commander left, Remy ran all the way home. He threw open the kitchen door. "What did you tell him?"

he shouted, out of breath, shaking his daughter by the arm. Anne was making bread, her hands trapped in the pull of dough.

"You must have known he was a spy."

Remy pushed Anne against the wall. She fell to her knees, shoulders hunched, lifted the ball of dough in front of her face, as if it were a shield.

"Get up," he said and slapped the dough away from Anne's face. Remy was roaring, lopsided. Anne tried to stand but her hands were useless, bound in the elastic of flour and water. She fell back to her knees.

"Get up," Remy said again and kicked her like a rabid dog. The web of dough stuck to Anne's hair, her eyebrows. Remy grabbed her arm. "He killed your mother." His breath was hot on her face.

Anne could see herself in her father's eyes. Such a failure. Now a traitor.

"Were you his whore?" Tears ran down Remy's face. "Answer me, girl. Has he come to claim his whore?"

Anne knew he wouldn't believe anything she said. The smell of yeast and tobacco and stale chocolate was overwhelming.

"It was not like that, Papa," she said, sobbing. The words shuddered even as she spoke them.

Remy threw himself away from her, as if she had suddenly burst into flames. In the moment, he became dark like the sky, low and angry.

"Then you cannot love me."

The clouds broke. The shock of his fist. The taste of blood in her mouth. The wrestle of love, not love.

Anne fled to the convent, the convent where the Commander now stands, nearly a year later, unaware that Anne is so close.

The smell of Shalimar still haunts him.

6

MUDDIED AND EXHAUSTED BEYOND LANGUAGE, Marie Claire, Anne, and Mother Xavier make their way to the convent in Tournai. The taste of lichen, sour in their mouths. Silent past border guards. Then onto a dairy cart, covered with straw, wedged between the metal milk cans, cool to the cheek. The horses, their uneven gait, bump and bruise and rattle. Then again on foot.

They must be careful. Very careful. Mother Xavier knows how the unraveling begins. Remembers it in nightmares. Questions like moths.

It is not until they arrive outside Tournai that Mother Xavier begins to see the impossibility of Marie Claire's situation. The child was buried for days yet shows no physical evidence of it. She is thin, yes, but no thinner than others whom the Sisters of His Divine and Most Sacred Blood have rescued. Marie Claire's belly is not bloated. In fact, the girl looks as if she's been at a picnic and has fallen into a slick of mud.

The inconsistency unnerves the nun.

"Let us wait here until sunset," she says, pointing toward the grove of figs that she's cultivated. The thicket of trees lies in a field that sits in the shadow of the convent, tucked into the bend of the river. A perfect place to hide. Branches reach out for each other like hands, provide cover for the women. Small green leaves sprout, as if unsure.

"It isn't season, no one will be there."

Last year when the soldiers arrived, they stripped the trees bare, breaking the branches, eating the fruit greedily.

From the window of her room, Mother Xavier could see them. She had heard that the soldiers were nearly starving. Forced to eat whatever they could find. She tried not to look at their faces, faces that reminded her of her own.

In the safety of the grove, the warm smell of wet bark makes Anne tired. She lays Marie Claire in a thatch of leaves. Kisses her forehead. "Sleep now," she says, barely able to keep her own eyes open.

Mother Xavier watches the scene, so domestic. Be careful, Anne, she thinks. Of what she isn't sure. A pain shoots down her chest, pulling her to one side. Tightens.

"Sister Anne," she calls out gently, not to alarm. Feels her breath go shallow.

Anne turns and sees the Reverend Mother's distress. This

can't go on, she thinks. *She'll be dead within a week.* In the shifting light of leaves, Anne sees the yellowed milk of her eyes. The sweat on her upper lip.

Anne puts her arm around Mother Xavier's waist, takes her hand. "Here," she says, and carefully lowers her on the stone bench used for meditation. Her ribs feel frail as a cat's.

Mother Xavier sinks to the bench slowly, tries to adjust her body for relief. She leans to one side. The pain grows less. "That's better," she says.

"Is there anything I can do?" Anne asks.

"Just sit, my dear, and rest. Sit next to me, close. Sunset will be here soon."

Anne looks back at Marie Claire, who is sleeping not more than a few feet away.

"She'll be fine there," Mother Xavier says. "Sit."

Anne does, and for many moments, she and Mother Xavier share quiet companionship. Holding hands. Too tired to speak. Aching. The pain in Mother Xavier's chest softens.

From where they rest, the convent towers over them. With the setting sun in their eyes, the stone walls are dark as mountains. Tournai is beyond. The afternoon light, golden, laces through the new leaves. Raises a sweet smell. Heats the grove gently.

Anne is watching Marie Claire. Has not taken her eyes off of her. The child, indeed, is beautiful despite how filthy she is. Though streaked with mud, slats of herself shine through.

Her skin, the iridescence of pearls. Her blue black hair sparks like flint. And then, so odd, the smell of roses.

After a while Anne speaks. "Marie Claire reminds me of myself as a child," she says. "So alone. Needing so much love."

Mother Xavier remembers Anne as she once was, a frightened child holding tightly to the sleeve of her habit. "It is not hard to love a child who needs you," she says. "Not hard at all."

Anne lays her head on Mother Xavier's lap. "I still need you," she says.

The pressure of Anne's head on her lap makes both legs go numb, but Mother Xavier doesn't care. I'll always protect you, she thinks, takes a deep breath, brushes back a wayward curl that has once again slipped from underneath Anne's cornet. *The fury of your hair. Your willow heart, always bending to the point of breaking.*

The gentle rhythm of Anne's breath in sleep brings tears to Mother Xavier's eyes. How have we come to this moment? she thinks. This level of danger? This darkness?

The child is an angel of God.

The words make her grow cold. It is a phrase she has not thought of in a long time. A prophecy from Anne's mother. One she vowed never to speak of. *Was Minouche insane or blessed with divine madness? Is the child, this child, this Marie Claire, an angel of God?*

If so, what is to become of Anne?

As a child Anne hid in the closet, buried among the tangle of boots, umbrellas, and bright yellow slickers. "Don't let them find me," she told her father. The blush of her hair, red as burnt almonds, turned sour with sweat.

"Mama says they'll make me a saint."

On his hands and knees Remy tried to coax her out. "It must be dusty in there," he'd say, not knowing what else to say. A chocolate melted in his hand.

Anne covered her ears. Pushed back further into the closet. *Go away. God will hear. God will hear. I want a bicycle, a new baby doll, a fancy Sunday dress with shiny shoes, and a dog that will lick my face. Go away.*

Take someone else.

Remy called upon Mother Xavier to consult. Just thirty years old, she had quickly risen through the ranks of the convent and had been named the principal at the church school. She was greatly trusted by the parents of her parish.

"Children are often afraid of sainthood," she said, sitting behind her cluttered desk. The small dark office was hot, smelled of sawdust and incense. "They come to believe that if one is a saint, one must die tragically and young. Just think of young Saint Catherine and that spiked wheel. Very horrible way to die. She was pulled apart then beheaded. The idea frightens me and I've heard that story many times. Imagine what a sensitive child like Anne must think."

Remy shifted in the straight-backed chair, a child's chair.

The only chair in the room. He shook his head. "It's more than that." He felt like a giant. Knees nearly to his chest.

"Minouche, Anne's mother, sees angels. Sometimes, she says, they grow angry with her and beat her."

Mother Xavier felt her left eye twitch. The word "madness" kicked the corners of the room. Threw dust.

Remy cleared his throat, looked at his hands as he spoke. "It began in her third month of pregnancy. She pulled me to the round of her flesh to hear their laughter. 'The child is swimming with angels,' she told me. I didn't know what to say."

"Did you hear them?"

"No," Remy said to his knees. Straightened his vest. "Of course not."

Mother Xavier folded and unfolded her mole hands. "That in itself means nothing, you know," she said, took off her glasses, and began to clean them with her worn cotton handkerchief. "And these beatings?"

"No marks."

"Why would the angels beat your wife?"

Remy shrugged, looked at his hands. "I have no idea."

"I see," the Reverend Mother said, continuing to wipe her glasses with large round strokes. "Angels are often sent to correct, punish, and teach," she said. "That could explain the beatings."

"But my wife is a good Christian woman."

Mother Xavier pointed a crooked finger at Remy. So accustomed to chastising small children, she shook her head and clucked. "Now, Monsieur Mathot," she said, "I know that you and your wife have not been in church since the celebration of your marriage. Perhaps, *this* is the cause of the angels' rancor," she said, then looked at him, expectant, waiting for him to speak, to promise to rectify the situation, to attend regularly, perhaps even every day.

Remy, too preoccupied for guilt, began to feel a glimmer of hope. Perhaps Minouche was not insane.

"Then it is possible?" he said. "It is entirely possible that my wife does indeed speak with the angels?"

"In Tournai," Mother Xavier sighed, "anything divine is entirely possible. Expected. Encouraged, even." She put on her glasses. They had so many streaks, she could hardly see.

"Then my wife is fine?"

"That is a difficult question." Mother Xavier looked straight into Remy's eyes, shook her head. "While it is true that miracles are a way of life in this city, Minouche's angels seem different," she said. "Extreme somehow."

Remy understood. In Tournai, most divine acts were moderate, genial in nature. In fact, from what he had read in the papers, heard in the streets, he likened the visions of Tournai to paintings at an exhibition.

When the face of Jesus was seen in a potato or the Virgin Mary appeared in a sheet hanging from a clothesline, people wound around the block to see them, as one does fine art. Eventually, as it is with exhibitions, the visions went away. People went home. That was the nature of divinity in Tournai. It came and went.

But Minouche's angels seemed unwilling to leave, and, worst of all, unwilling to show themselves to anyone except her.

Mother Xavier stood. "The air in Tournai is so dense with visions, the Passion of our Lord. What harm does it do to desire so keenly to be a part of it that one sometimes imagines? Perhaps, if you attended church on a regular basis."

Remy stood. "Thank you for your time, Sister."

Mother Xavier reached across the desk and took his arm. "Monsieur Mathot, I caution you," she said, her voice stern. "Do not underestimate the need for grace in your life. If you do, it can only lead to unhappiness."

Remy, unaccustomed to such direct behavior, smiled at his hat, the quail feather tucked in its fold. "I am sure you are right, Mother Xavier," he said, and stood. The small chair rattled to the floor.

On the walk home, Remy told himself over and over again, everything is fine, just fine, and thought back to the time when he and Minouche first met. How he was taken by surprise with it all.

In a sense, Remy had never considered the idea of love. It was not that he objected to it, it was just that he had not scheduled time for it. Mathot & Sons was the finest purveyor of chocolates in all of Belgium. Perhaps, the world. Started by Remy's father, passed to him, it was family, lover, friend. His pride. The smell of chocolate from the factory smoothed the curtains in his bedroom. Lay softly against his cheek at night.

But Remy did not speak Italian, and that is how things changed. One day an order, which needed translation, arrived at the factory. Father Pascal was an expert in languages. In the cell of his rectory office, the parish priest and his favorite student, Minouche, worked diligently.

The sight of Minouche made Remy dizzy, lost within his own body. Her hair was the color of burnt almonds. Her skin like cream. All Remy knew about her was that she was an orphan who had a beautiful smile.

Minouche. Me-noo-sh. Mee-nooo-shh. Meee-noo-sh. For hours after he left, Remy said her name over and over again, emphasizing each syllable differently. He wanted to say it just right. Not too anxious. Not too familiar. Confident. Personable.

Remy was a man unaccustomed to the pull of something larger than himself. Once the wanting took hold, the accounting went undone. The testers were unsupervised, grew fat. Remy spent his days in the dairy room, slowly pouring cream into the copper vats. A silken waterfall. Its sheen brought tears to his eyes. The brown-faced men in rubber boots, hip-high, smoked Gitanes, drank too much beer for lunch, and laughed. Happy to have a boss who did their work for them. Cream curdling underneath his nails instead of theirs.

Remy and Minouche were wed on the eve of her sixteenth birthday. A year later, Anne, and the angels, arrived.

As Anne grew into a shy child, spindly, the angels visited Minouche more frequently, gave the family no peace. One day, Minouche told Remy that they sipped tea and talked at great length of the exquisite beauty of chocolate, its fine sheen, its gentle warmth on the lips. It is the one thing the angels said they could not get in heaven, she said.

While her mother spoke, Anne buried her head in her lap. Covered her ears. Hummed a single note until her body shook like a tuning fork.

"Everywhere they look they see chocolate," Minouche said. "It is their nature, this longing."

Remy began to lock himself in his study at night. Sometimes it hurt to breathe.

Something must be done. He knew it was true, but Minouche was so beautiful and, of course, there was little Anne to consider.

"Is it madness or divinity?" he asked Mother Xavier once more. "I must know." He paced back and forth in her office. "You must tell me."

Mother Xavier shuffled the pages on her desk. The stories of Minouche and her angels were becoming widespread, and even more extreme.

"I have not seen you in mass," she said. "I would think you should ask God's assistance in matters such as these."

"Just tell me if it's possible."

Remy leaned across her desk. It rocked back and forth.

Mother Xavier studied his eyes. Dust hung in the air. "Have you read of Emanuel Swedenborg?" she said. "The scientist? Eighteenth century? Swedish?"

Remy shook his head. "What does he have to do with my wife?" He was nearly shouting.

Mother Xavier stood. "He said that angels spoke to him, and many believed him." She folded her hands in front of her.

Remy took a step back. Looked at the nun closely. "Was it true?"

"The American, Johnny Appleseed, buried pages of Swedenborg's books along with seeds."

"But was it true?"

"Why don't you ask God?" she said softly. "It is not right for a man of your stature to avoid worship. Think of the child. What example do you set?"

Remy felt the words like a slap. "Just tell me if it's possible."

"In Tournai, anything is possible."

"Then why can't I see these angels myself?"

Mother Xavier leaned across the desk, took Remy's hand in hers. "You must ask God," she said sadly. "I'm sorry. Only He has the answer. I'm very sorry."

So Remy went to the church. Knelt at the front altar, and prayed every prayer he had ever been taught. Soon, the prayers became the question "Is she mad or divine?" and the question was all he could think to pray. Hours and hours passed. The question remained. Remy prayed until he had lost feeling in his knees, until he could not stand the smell of his own sweat. He prayed for nearly two days and then he left.

God never answers.

But He did.

Summer. In the heat of noon, the angels visited Minouche as she shopped in the town square. Much of the parish watched as she talked to the air. Laughed at imaginary jokes. Anne walked alongside her mother, flat-faced and drained, pulling out her pale eyelashes, one by one.

Mother Xavier called for Remy at his factory. When he saw her, his hands began to sweat.

"I'm concerned for little Anne," she said. "So pale, she was, like a sleepwalker."

Remy listened to the details until he couldn't bear to listen anymore. He ran through the cracked field to his house. The day's heat had made everything brittle, white-knuckled. Even though it was now late afternoon, the sun was sharper than usual. As Remy came closer to the house, he could see that every window was closed. The shutters locked. The curtains pulled. *It must be stifling.* He ran up the front stairs.

"Minouche!" he shouted, as he threw open the double doors. His voice cracking. The brass knocker bounced. He stood in the hallway for just a moment. The house seemed to be completely empty.

"Anne?"

Remy shouted down the hallway. His voice echoed. He shouted from the entryway to his study to the kitchen to the dining room. He ran up the winding staircase, two steps at a time.

Upstairs the hallway was dark. At first glance, Remy thought the doors to all the rooms were closed, but as his eyes adjusted, he noticed that the door to the sitting room was slightly open. Through the crack he could see the flickering of a candle, dust reflected in its light.

Finally.

The door creaked as he opened it. A gust of stifled air, sticky sweet, swept over him. *What is that smell?* Minouche sat alone in the window seat reading the Bible. The curtains were drawn. The small cross around her neck reflected the candlelight, like a beacon. Remy could hardly catch his breath. Heat rose from the floor. The room was oddly calm.

"I've been looking all over for you," he said, panting, sitting on the edge of the horsehair cushion. Sweat beaded off his forehead. Minouche's feet were tucked underneath her as if they were cold, but the room was hot, too hot.

"Where's Anne?"

Minouche didn't look up, continued reading as if Remy wasn't there. Remy noticed she was wearing her black wool cardigan from the hall closet, wrapped tightly around her.

"Are you ill?"

The sour smell in the air was stronger near Minouche. Sticky, familiar. He held his breath, as if she were contagious.

"Can you hear me?"

Remy noticed that she wasn't reading the entire page, but a paragraph, the same paragraph, over and over again. Her fingers ran along the words as if they were Braille. Hebrews 13:2.

Be not forgetful to entertain strangers for thereby some have entertained angels unaware.

Under her breath, she said the phrase over and over again, as if trying to make sense of it. Remy took her chin into his hand. Her finger slipped from the passage.

"The child saved will be an angel of God," she said, the words a rumble. "When they spoke, the light was blinding."

"When who spoke? The angels?"

"The child saved will be an angel of God."

"What child? Anne? Is Anne the child?"

Minouche's breath was hard and shallow.

What is that smell? Remy held his breath again and pulled Minouche's face close to his. Her eyes were dull, unfocused. I love you, he thought. He moved to kiss her lips. She turned away.

"These angels," he said, quietly, speaking to the Bible in Minouche's lap. "We must have them go away. You say they want chocolate. If they've come for chocolate, I shall close the factory and they will leave. No?"

Minouche's breath turned quick, like a metronome.

"Please," he said. "I don't know what to do anymore." He laid his head on his wife's lap, as if he were a child. "Tell me what to do," he said.

Remy felt a drop run down his forehead, thought it to be a bit of her sweat. *It is too warm for that cardigan. Boiled wool.* The drop rolled into Remy's eye, stinging. And then another. And another. Remy rubbed his face. Looked at his hand. Streaked.

Slowly, Remy moved away from his wife, backward into the moment, as if it were already a memory, a bad dream. He looked at his hand again.

Blood.

Minouche's cardigan fell open. A tangle of rose thorns were wrapped tightly across her tender breasts. Pounded in deep. The silk of her blouse made delicate with blood.

She is quietly bleeding to death.

Remy felt his heart beat faster, mouth go metallic.

"The angel of God will come for Anne," she said. "And the miracles will begin." Then she lost consciousness.

Anne was nowhere to be found.

Search parties cast their lights low over the forest floor. *How much tragedy can one man take?* many thought. After hours of searching the grounds, the factory, no luck.

Drowned.

Kidnapped.

Murdered.

Mother Xavier offered comfort. Brought Remy hot coffee with equal parts of milk. A sprinkle of cinnamon. "I'm sorry," she said, wanted to say so much more.

Someone shouted his name.

Remy ran from her as fast as he could.

It was midnight when everyone gave up, went home. They said they would return tomorrow. Tomorrow, they said, they'd bring the dogs. Shovels.

Shovels?

Remy didn't want to think of the implications of the word. *Midnight.* The bells of the cathedrals began to toll, peal, and clang. Four hundred bells, each one ringing. Each ring sounding, overlaid one upon another upon another. The booming fat bells of St. Mark's, clangers as big as a man. The high tinny bells of St. Agnes. The clear, sweet peal of Our Lady. Four hundred bells. Praising. Beseeching. Testifying. A roaring cacophony vying for God's love.

Minouche. Me-noosh. Mee-nooo-shh. Meee-noosh.

All he could hear was her name.

Remy was curled in the great hall of his house, on the cold marble floor. He cried without tears, open-mouthed and gasping. He could not imagine his life anymore. Without Minouche. Without Anne. *Shovels.* The buckle of his raincoat pushed into his rib. Hard metal. Unyielding.

He was afraid to sleep. How could he dream?

There is nothing left.

The moon slid across the room, half breathing. Cautiously,

the light shifted. Remy noticed there was a pile of sawdust in the corner of the room. An oak molding half-eaten away. *Termites*. He moved in closer to watch them, their pale bodies, their mindless industry. *Such perfect businessmen.*

Remy knew he couldn't lie there forever. This is a very nice raincoat, he told himself, an admonishment. *Which must be put away.*

He stood, uneasy. His hand on the closet door. His imagination supplied the details. Minouche, the thorns wrapped tightly around her breasts, opened this closet to take out her favorite cardigan. Black. Boiled wool. Wrapped it around her wounds. *What was she thinking?* Remy took a hanger. Stiff-necked, it slipped, rattled to the floor. He bent to pick it up. The light shifted.

Anne.

For a moment, Remy thought he was imagining it. Dreaming madness. In the tangle of coats and shoes, the pallor of Anne's skin, so like her mother's. Like cream, he thought, laughed, wanted to shout. *She is fine. Something of my life has been spared.*

Anne's breathing was heavy and fitful in sleep. Remy didn't want to startle her. He untangled her as one does tissue from fruit. Easily bruised. Anne was unscathed. Remy felt the warmth of luck, like embers.

She was right here, safe, all night.

Carefully, Remy carried Anne up to her room. "I love you," he said, kissed her forehead, tucked her blankets up under her chin. The small cloth dog, threadbare, placed so gently into the crook of her arm.

Half-awake, she turned to him. "Shh," she said. "The angels will hear."

"I won't let them take you," he said. But when the time came he had no choice in the matter.

And neither did Mother Xavier.

7

THE SKY IS RED.

In the shadow of the convent, the air is sour with fog, the humic acid of the river.

The moon, gray silk.

"It is time," Mother Xavier says. They make their way up the hill, slowly, quietly.

In the street, in front of the convent, a convoy of trucks rumble down the hill into Tournai. Two soldiers stand idle outside the convent's gate, saluting. Cigarettes flare hidden in the cupped hands behind their backs. Their heads bob in blue clouds.

Hiding in the shadow of the convent, Mother Xavier sees the men, the trucks. She gently pulls Anne, still carrying the sleeping Marie Claire, into the tangle of underbrush near the river's edge.

"Do you think they know?" Anne whispers. From that distance, Anne can see that there are soldiers, just two. One of them turns toward them, the bushes in which they are hiding, but just as quickly, turns back to the convoy, salutes the passing trucks.

"I don't think so," Mother Xavier says. She can see the narrow ledge behind the convent, the coal chute door. *Safety, so close*. "But the trucks provide a good distraction," she says. Anne nods.

Not more than a few feet away, the Commander is hiding. Crouched on the edge of the river, in a cradle of brambles. In the gray twilight, all he can clearly see is the shape of two nuns, not their faces. One is carrying a child in her arms. The small one must be Mother Xavier, he thinks. *The child, most certainly a Jew*. He can hear them breathe, the rustling of their habits, the prickly bushes against the cloth.

The Commander steadies himself. He has lost all feeling in his legs but will not kneel in the mud. *It is unbecoming*. He is so tired, he grinds his teeth. Since his arrival in Tournai, he knows his loyalty has come into question. The townspeople who remember his affair with Anne still speak of it in the streets, where his soldiers laugh at his foolishness, make reports to his superiors. The Commander knows he has to prove himself if he wants to avoid a charge of treason. To uncover

the base of operations for the Resistance, single-handedly—
that will win favor, he thinks.

Marie Claire, still sleeping, gently touches Anne's face as if
reaching out to her in a dream. Such beauty, Anne thinks, and
holds the child closer. For a moment, it's as if she is Anne's
child, the sweat of her hair, the muddied skin, the grid of
scratches, are part of Anne's own flesh. *Innocent. Needy. Loved.*

"We are here," Anne whispers to Marie Claire. "We are
finally here." Still half-asleep, Marie Claire unfurls. Falters.
Her legs, new as a colt's. "Steady. Steady," Anne says. The
child is all elbows and knees, easing herself onto the cracked
ground. She rubs her eyes.

"Everything is all right," Mother Xavier says, brushes back
a thatch of muddied hair woven with twigs, leaves, the down
from a small bird. "We'll get you clean in no time. We're
home now." The creak of her bedsprings. The bleach of her
worn muslin sheets. Home.

"It's not as big as it looks," Anne joins in. "But it's twice
as cold!"

A clanging voice, Mother Xavier thinks. Not Anne's own,
too bright. A voice for children. Something she must have
remembered a nanny doing. Mother Xavier is annoyed by this
odd tone. Grating. Soon, she fears, Anne will revert to baby
talk.

The Commander can smell the salt of Marie Claire's sweat.
How very easy this is, he thinks.

Anne gently pushes the child deeper into the thicket of branches. "You'll be safer here," she says.

The Commander quietly lifts the gun from its holster. The heavy steel is cool in his hand. A cloud passes. The moon reflects off the nun's cornets, starched and ready for flight. *It's a clear shot.*

"I'll go first," Anne says, "I'll run toward the chute. If I make it, wait a couple of minutes, then follow."

Anne quickly removes her boots, her wool socks. The ground has the ice of spring-late-in-coming. Barefoot, she knows she can remain silent, undetected. "I'll go down the chute first, then you can slide Marie Claire," she says. Mother Xavier nods.

Marie Claire begins to shiver, as if she is cold. Mother Xavier leans into the child, holds her in her arms. "It's all right," she says. "I've slid down that chute myself." Marie Claire doesn't seem to be listening, watches Anne intently.

You'll be fine, Mother Xavier says, looks at the child, then away, her eyes searching the horizon, the convent, the grove of figs, the river pushing its rocks, silently, back and forth. There's something about this child, she thinks. Like the blue of flame. Cool. Luminescent. *And the smell of roses.* Mother Xavier noticed it when Anne first lifted Marie Claire from the root cellar. Now, as the hours since her rescue are organized into a day, the smell still remains. When the child was asleep, it seemed even stronger. *How odd.*

No matter, Mother Xavier thinks. In two days' time, the Resistance will move Marie Claire downriver to a safe house, then on to Israel or a family in Switzerland. That is how it is usually done. At least, that's the plan. *But still. How could a child survive without food?* Mother Xavier feels her own stomach knead like bread.

"Don't go," Marie Claire says, grabs Anne's sleeve.

"Don't worry, you'll follow me."

"It's not safe."

"I've done it before."

The Commander steadies the gun with his left hand. He has been waiting for this moment so long, he's filled with a profound sense of pleasure. *These nuns take me for a fool.*

Marie Claire reaches toward Anne again, but Anne takes a step back. "I have to go," she says. The child's hand hangs in the air a moment, fingers grow cold. For some reason, perhaps exhaustion, Anne thinks of her father. Just out of reach. His house, the factory, down the hill from the convent. She's not seen him since she came. *Probably better that way.*

"It's all right," she says to Marie Claire, hears her father's voice instead of her own. Two weeks after her mother entered the hospital, Remy still would not leave his study. No one knew when her mother would return.

"It's all right," he'd say. "It's all right." The brass lock between them.

Anne thinks to hold Marie Claire's frail hand, but doesn't. Turns abruptly. Runs while she still can.

The Commander sees a nun move toward the convent, toward the coal chute, still propped open with the wooden wedge. I knew it, he thinks, and cocks his head, ever so slightly, like a cat. As a marksman, he has the tendency to pull to the right. He has to compensate.

Marie Claire watches Anne move across the landscape. The dried leaf of sunset is slowly falling to the ground. For just a moment, the night wind catches Anne's habit, a dark sail in the red sky. Marie Claire watches, her mouth slightly open. Without sound, yet moving, as if she is speaking in someone else's dream.

"We'll join her soon," Mother Xavier says. Her knees are dumb with pain. She sits hard on the ground, pulls Marie Claire into her lap. The child pulls away, slightly.

The Commander smiles. When he fires, the gun jumps in his hand.

The bullet catches Anne's arm. It moves against her skin like a match. Just a graze, she thinks, stumbles but keeps running. Anne's mind is a jumble of prayer. Inside her pocket is a rosary. Her fingers work the perfect pearl beads. The acid taste in her mouth.

Mother Xavier cannot breathe. *He is ten feet away, maybe less.* The smell of roses swells in her throat. Damn you, she thinks, unflinching. Mother Xavier pulls the child, herself, flat onto the ground. In this moment, the scene comes back to her.

The moonlight. The Commander's steel eyes. The raft. Sister Ruth tossed across it, lifeless, haphazard, slipping with each wave. Her legs twisted, as if to run. The slack of her hand opened as if in offering.

So loved.

The Commander takes aim again.

The soldiers, cigarettes out, turn their attention to the river, the sound of the shot. "Who's there?" the youngest one shouts, his German guttural. In the darkness he can see nothing.

Marie Claire rolls out from underneath Mother Xavier and runs fast, low to the ground toward the Commander. The grace of a hunting dog, wild with instinct and focus.

Anne wants to pray but the words will not come. *Our Father? Hail Mary? Blessed art thou?* As she runs along the convent wall, all she can remember are fragments of prayers.

This time he won't miss.

The ledge crumbles beneath Anne's feet. She swings the door of the coal chute open. The stone of the convent wall flakes, falls to the ground like ash. Anne jumps, head first— bangs and bruises along the steel chute—falls onto the floor of the basement. Her wrists bend but do not break. Her shoulder is bleeding and burns. *Dear God*, she begins, takes the rosary from her pocket. Her body shakes and she prays.

Save them. Please, save them.

Marie Claire lunges at the Commander, catches him off guard. His gun falls from his hand into a bush. Marie Claire is all nails and teeth. A violent universe, evolving. The Commander can't defend himself. His legs are numb, useless.

Stupid child.

The two roll closer to the river's edge, out of sight in the tangle of undergrowth. From where the soldiers stand, at the edge of the street, they can see nothing in the dark. "What is that?" the younger says. "Did you hear a shot?"

"Maybe a truck," the other says, checks his watch. Their shift is nearly over. Soon, it will not be their problem. They turn their attention back to the street.

The Commander slaps Marie Claire in the face. Her head snaps back. He would shout out to his men, but *how embarrassing*. She's just a child. A Jew. *They'll laugh at me even more.* His bloodless legs are useless. He can smell the river. He lifts Marie Claire over his head and shakes her like a rag doll.

Mother Xavier sees the girl, her head above the tangle of bushes. Her clear eyes. Open mouth. The bruised pale of her face.

No . . .

In the street, she hears the click of the soldier's metal boots as they walk away. Propelled by fear and heat and anger, an anger she has never known, Mother Xavier lunges toward the Commander. Her glasses fall to the ground, tangle under her feet. Her world slips out of focus. She picks up a rock and hits him hard, very hard. The side of his head bleeds. She hits him again. An eye. And again.

The taste of blood surprises him. He thought this would be easy, the capture of women.

With one dark push, Mother Xavier rolls him into the river. The Commander's legs are useless, the current is swift. In the street his men are laughing, unaware. The splash of his body goes unheard.

Mother Xavier can think of no prayer to say, feels she has no time to ask for forgiveness, *at any moment he could shout*, but instead of running she picks up her broken glasses, now bent beyond repair, and watches him roll down the hill into the water. Just to be sure.

Marie Claire is half-curled in the dirt. A cub, waiting for the wolf to return. Mother Xavier tosses her broken glasses into the river. *No matter.* She knows this river. This convent. This life. The dullness of its nicked edge. Quickly, she takes off her cornet, her veil. Her hair, newly gray. She lifts Marie Claire into her arms and covers the child with the length of brown wool. The cornet, its wings of white linen, is discarded.

As Mother Xavier runs with the child in her arms, every second is lived, as if without breath. The night seems to pull her along. The river's edge, its tangle of trees and under-growth, rip at her habit. Without hesitation, she runs across the narrow ledge behind the convent. Stones slip beneath her feet, roll into the water, splash louder than they should. She watches the dirt beneath her feet shift. The ledge is nearly gone, eroded into the current. Thou shall not kill, she thinks, Thou shall not kill.

Her breath, the words, her feet pounding on the soft grass—all become one. *Thou shall not kill*. The coal chute door is still propped open, the way Anne left it.

Mother Xavier strokes Marie Claire's forehead, a sign of the cross, then pushes her down the cold steel slide in a cloud of silt. Mother Xavier sneezes, her head jerks back. She rocks back and forth on the edge of eroding grass. Twenty-five feet straight down. Then rapids. Her brown wool veil, once wrapped around the child, falls into the river, is pulled, frantic, downstream. She feels herself slipping backward. Grabs the coal chute door.

What have I done?

The moon turns away, casts the night in the light of granite.

8

THE COMMANDER HITS THE WATER HARD, AS IF it were a wall. Bone to stone. Crumbling. The river, its rapids, undefined in its anger, beats his body like one of its rocks. Matted wheat of hair. Blood, like a pulse. His right eye is swelling. His skin is paper, wrapped in nerve. He is being dragged backward in the current, a school of fish part around him—the useless legs, the arms so bruised they are unable to grasp.

Time slows. He tells himself that he is not going to panic. *I am not drowning.* Once again, the scum of the water fills his mouth. He gags, can't catch his breath.

Overhead, the sound of a fighter, low on fuel, follows the river to the sea, to England. The Commander hears the plane cough and spit. He imagines that on its nose there is a painted lady. "My Dream Girl" it says. The Commander believes she is smiling at him. A sultry beauty queen in a black evening dress, low cut and clinging. A cigarette holder in one hand. He can hear the fighter bank a turn, steep. Nearly loses control. The throat of the engine sputters, sucking gas.

In a split second, above the airplane, the Commander sees a flash of light, like a camera. And then another. It is the moon reflecting off the propellers of twin fighters. The gray and green, he thinks. *Luftwaffe*. Their dark rumble, steady, sounds as if they are hanging above the beauty queen for just a moment. Suspended in a starless sky, she waves to him. They zero in. The cream of her skin.

Good for us, he thinks.

9

INSIDE THE CONVENT, ANNE IS KNEELING ON THE sharp coal, breathing hard, waiting for Marie Claire with outstretched arms. The blood from Anne's wound runs down her shoulder and under her arm in a thin stream, gives her goose bumps, but she doesn't wipe it away, doesn't move. In the darkness, she hears the child tumble sideways. She is coming, coming to her new home, she thinks. *The convent is so big, too big. Chapel. Mother house. Stone, all stone. No place for a child.*

The first day Anne arrived comes back to her, wedges in her throat. The echo of her voice in prayer, the hollow heart of her room. Single bed. Sheets wrapped tight. The wooden cross. Jesus, whose eyes see all.

Now her room is a clutter of cards, greeting cards, hanging on the walls on thick rusted nails, old yellowed tape; stuffed into chocolate boxes under the bed; tumbling off the top of the bed and jammed into drawers. Cards stick out of every crack and crevice like tufts of fur.

They have never been sent.

"Joyeux Noel!" The laughing snowman waves to no one in particular. *"Souhaits Sincères!"* The words twine together with lilies of the field, their bells unmoving.

Anne imagines who could receive these cards—people she doesn't know, people she knew before the war. *"Meilleurs Voeux"* for the baker, lean as dried sheets, covered in flour. His mother, her stray eye, always watching. *"Joyeuses Pâques"* for the African beggar from Martinique, taken away one night by soldiers, in a garden, betrayed by a friend. He said he was a tribal prince, sang trancelike in the city square, hoping for a bit of coin to fall into his turban.

"Porte Bonheur!" "Mammy Décédée!" Birth cards. Death cards. Waiting. All waiting. Like Anne.

He taught her to draw. He was, after all, an artist.

Marie Claire rolls toward Anne like hard labor, thunder giving birth, banging the sides of the steel chute. She lets out a sharp cry. Anne flinches. She must be bleeding, she thinks. *There'll be a scar, a wound. Closer. Closer. There. A hand, a head.* The child tumbles into Anne's arms. *Finally.*

"You are safe." Anne kisses the child on both cheeks. Marie Claire begins to cry. Anne knows nothing of children. Her palms sweat.

"I'm sorry," Anne says, doesn't know what else to say.

Imagines a card with a stork. A top hat. A cigar. Lace scallops the edges.

"How do I know if I have died?" Marie Claire whispers, as if it is a secret. Her breath is cool, a small sweet plum.

"You are fine," Anne says, and brushes back a strand of muddied hair. *It must be shock.* Gray fog, like old jelly. *So much has happened to us all.*

Anne presses Marie Claire close, carries her to the nearby laundry room. No blood, she thinks, but the child's face is badly bruised. Around her small neck, the outline of two hands swells to the surface. Purple and black fingers.

We have to hurry, Anne says.

Marie Claire is so filthy, her clothes, so caked with mud and coal, they wrap her body like a wasp's nest. Anne lifts her, clothes and all, into a laundry tub still filled with water. Bits of coal and dust film the surface. Even the bar of soap turns black. The water softens the mud just enough. Gently, Anne unbuttons Marie Claire's dress, takes it back to the coal room, throws it into the furnace. When she returns, Marie Claire is sitting in the tub, hugging her knees. Her body is so coated in mud, modesty is not an issue.

Mother Xavier opens the door to the damp room, sees the filthy water, the filthy child, Anne covered with soot. "More water is needed," she says, quietly, to no one in particular. Anne half expects her to fetch some, but she does not.

Moments pass in uncomfortable silence. Mother Xavier rubs her forearms, as if she is cold. How can I tell Anne? she thinks.

"We have to hurry, they'll be here soon," Anne says.

Mother Xavier clears her throat. "I don't think so," she says, the words sound weak.

"What do you mean?"

"I believe he acted alone."

"Yes, but."

"I believe he is dead, the Commander."

The words hang unblinking between the two women.

"I saw him drown."

Somewhere in the hallway, Anne hears a mouse. The tiny clatter of its jagged claws.

I believe he is dead.

Anne's mind feels like a vast hall, cool and empty. The last time she saw him they sat in Le Madrigal, her uncle's restaurant. Knees touching. Chairs balanced on tabletops. They were alone, the champagne finished, the restaurant long closed, waiting for the sunrise. He said he was an artist, not a soldier, not a commander. Perhaps he was. She had no reason not to believe him. The wheat of his hair, his clear eyes.

"I know how you felt about him."

"Maybe there's a mistake."

Mother Xavier shakes her head. "I saw his body float down-river. I'm sorry."

"How is it possible?" Anne asks. All she can think about is the color of his cheek in candlelight. The taste of strawberries, heat-ripened.

"It was an accident." Mother Xavier moves to touch Anne's cheek, a sign of comfort, but Anne moves away from her.

"He tried to kill Marie Claire." She stops and coughs, clears her throat. Her voice turns hoarse. "He slipped and fell."

"How is that possible? Weren't you with Marie Claire? Couldn't you have saved him?"

Mother Xavier won't meet Anne's eye. "Perhaps I could have, but we would have all been exposed.

"I had no choice, please forgive me."

"I don't understand."

Anne bites her lower lip. The lie settles uneasily between them. One sorrow piles upon the next.

With a deep breath, Mother Xavier eases herself slowly onto an old wooden bench. Splinters slide into the dark brown wool of her habit. The pain in her lower back has become unbearable, made worse by the struggle, and then landing tailbone first on top of the coal heap. She had not planned to come that way, but given the circumstances, she had no choice. She sits carefully on the edge of the bench, her shoulders hunched, and runs a hand though her hair. A gray strand falls onto her lap.

I have become Them, she thinks, a liar, a killer. *Just like Them.* They, Them: her parents. Mother Xavier no longer thinks of them as Mother and Father, or even by their Christian names. To her, they have become a sorrow so deep, she cannot name it. The Resistance knows the Kepplers work for the

Third Reich, believes they're involved with highly experimental studies. Genetics. That is all that is known. Mother Xavier believes it, too. She suspects, from the letters that the soldiers deliver—the letters that only speak of weather and bunions and poorly cooked food—that their work is very important. Fears the details. Prays for their souls. Subverts their efforts.

Since the war began, Mother Xavier and the sisters have been the cornerstone of the Resistance. They have saved so many, hidden so many. The catacombs are littered with the things those rescued have left behind. Clothes. Shoes. A wooden top. The convent has become a place where people shed their old lives. A port, not a destination.

Sometimes, when everyone is asleep, Mother Xavier balances herself on the sea of these things. Pricks her palms, the tops of her feet, with a sewing needle. Enraptured by the moment, teasing stigmata, she waits for a sign of forgiveness for herself and her parents, especially her parents, but the tiny drops of blood hesitate, embarrassed, slip down the center of her palms, follow the groove of her life line. The line is long, so long it extends all the way around the heel of her palm.

No luck. No vision. No salvation. No rapture of ecumenical joy. Just tiny drops of blood, drying without dignity. She sucks them away before anyone sees them.

God has forsaken us all, she thinks, watching Anne and the child. Without her glasses, the steam seems to enfold them, like a halo. Marie Claire, no longer shivering, reaches up to touch the tear in Anne's habit where the bullet grazed her shoulder. Her tiny fingers, water beading off them like spring rain off lilies of the valley.

Anne catches Marie Claire's hand and holds it as if it were sacred, a bit of bread. The body, the blood. Tears drop into the stale water.

Was my mother ever like this to me, Mother Xavier thinks. *Did we have this moment? This gentleness?*

I have no memory of it.

The words well in her throat, she looks away. Removes a shoe. The leather at the toes is cracked, the color of dust. And then the other: its sole, a canyon of miles, eroded. She gently removes her rough wool socks. Slowly, she stands, lifts her habit, fingers its fraying hem, the mended side pocket. She takes the rosary from her pocket, kisses its wooden cross, as if by rote, weaves the beads between her fingers.

Mother Xavier is shedding like a snake.

The water in the tub gently laps at the metal sides. Marie Claire is lifted, wrapped in a towel. Mother Xavier in the worn weave of her flannel chemise, a cloud. She watches as Anne carefully dries Marie Claire, watches as one who watches fellow passengers on a train. Anne holds Marie Claire, half-covered in thick cotton. *It is time to go.* "Peace be with you," she says to Mother Xavier.

Mother Xavier doesn't answer. She lowers herself to the ground. The bone pink of knees. The nakedness of it.

Anne looks away, wanting to be invisible. To live life unnoticed, as a thought.

Mother Xavier lies flat on the stone floor, prostrate for forgiveness. It is the custom of the order, but her body looks thrown there, cast aside. She has killed a man, lied about it, but will not pray for forgiveness. How can she? she thinks. She no longer knows who to pray to. He in His infinite wisdom? He, so willing to fill the world with that which is evil and base? He, who withholds the miraculous, punishes the good, betrays the just? He, this creature who demands love to be given openly, freely, without reservation and yet sets forth impossible rules for us to follow to win His silent approval? He the invisible. He the almighty. He the unforgiving.

Bits of dirt press into Mother Xavier's cheek. Her almond hands, like Ruth's, are open. Blue rivers. Upstairs, in Mother Xavier's office, there is a letter from her parents, just recently delivered by the Commander himself.

The Polish postmark made her mouth go sour. The letter says they'll be near Tournai, somewhere in France, tomorrow, looking for a new facility. *Tomorrow.*

Could they come to talk?

10

REMY IS USUALLY CAREFUL, VERY CAREFUL WHEN he makes his delivery to the convent. Many have been shot after curfew, he knows that. Not just Jews. He knows that. His palms sweat. The stone streets are slick under his feet, making it impossible to run without slipping. Whenever a cloud slides over the moon, a milky screen, Remy runs from doorway to doorway. His feet slide. He catches himself and runs some more.

It is fifteen doorways to the church, he counts them every week. Then a steep run uphill to the convent. No cover. That's the dangerous part. He has no choice. The delivery must be made.

For Remy, the stakes had become higher than he could imagine. He knows from Father Pascal that Anne and the sisters work with the Resistance. He wants to help them any way he can, but he can't. It would be too dangerous. Since the occupation, the fame of Mathot & Sons has grown, although not in the way he desired.

"Collaborator," his old friends hiss under their breath. Spit on his only remaining pair of good shoes. Only Father Pascal, the parish priest, would speak to him, and then not publicly.

Chocolates are the one thing left in his life. The only thing valuable he can give to Anne.

The only thing left.

The pink box is tucked under his arm. The ribbon is beginning to unravel. This week there are only caramel centers, some of which are slightly bitter. No flavored creams. No fruit, even though Remy knows it is Anne's favorite. Fruit has become too dear and too dangerous. The soldiers pick the early berries themselves, feel territorial about what is not theirs.

One more doorway.

When he hears the shot fired by the Commander, he is standing in the doorway of a furniture repair shop. A moment before, he has seen himself reflected in the mirror of a rosewood dresser. He was surprised. His hair has grown down to his shoulders. Gray as webs, spun, then abandoned. It's been weeks since he's shaven, since he's seen himself so closely. Much has changed. His faces sags, like wax.

The church doorway is next. He hears the shot fired. The shot comes from the top of the hill.

Anne.

Remy runs without thinking toward the church door. From there he knows he can see the convent at the top of the hill, see what may or may not have happened. It could be nothing, he tells himself in an effort at calm. He runs along the wet street, his feet slipping. *It could be nothing at all.*

Remy holds the box of chocolates tightly to his chest. The church is always the hardest door to pass. His body flush, leaning against it, he often imagines Father Pascal standing on the other side. He thinks of the priest's face, so like his father's. His voice, like his father's.

Remy doesn't see the caravan of German trucks and tanks until it is too late.

"Hey, you!"

Remy runs up the church stairs two steps at a time. The night air makes them slick as oil. Halfway up, his foot slips.

"Stop!"

Remy falls hard, hard, rolls. The box of chocolates are tucked tightly into his coat. The steps are unrelenting as a boxer, bruising his head, his face, chipping his front tooth. At the bottom of the stairs, the metal railing cracks the bridge of his nose, drives the bone and cartilage up though the gray of his brain.

A truck slows down. A soldier jumps out of the passenger's side.

At the bottom of the stairs, Remy lies in a pool of his own

blood. My head, he thinks. Then the moment slips out of focus, rocks back and forth like a ship on high seas.

Above him, the church door cracks open a bit. Yellow light behind a stooped figure. *Father Pascal.* Remy knows it is him. He can almost smell the acid of the old man's sweat mixed with sweet grape wine. He wants to call out but the door closes before he can speak.

The soldier stands over Remy, kicks him in the face.

Remy blinks and blinks, uncontrollable. Urine runs down his pant leg, warms the fold of his silk sock. For a moment, language escapes him. He thinks without the splints of words; thought without form or restrictions. The world is muted and bright at the same time.

Blood is seeping into his brain.

In that moment, when everything is quiet and loud and bright and dark, Remy hears a metal click. The last bit of his life recognizes it, can process its meaning. He feels the cold metal of the barrel against his head.

I am sorry, Anne.

Feels nothing else.

The box of chocolates falls into the street.

11

WHO IS DEAD? WHO IS NOT? IN TIMES OF WAR this is a critical question. The body count is always important, that's how victories are decided.

But how can you tell if one is truly dead?

Yes, after the soldier left, Remy had no pulse. His heart no longer beat.

Wheezing, Father Pascal drags his lifeless body up the fourteen stairs to the church door. The backs of Remy's good shoes bump and scratch along the stone steps. The body, heavy. The old priest, dizzy. He pauses on the stoop to catch his breath and make a mental note to remove the shoes before Remy is buried. They are almost his size, Italian leather, soft and nearly new.

Father Pascal straightens his vestments, drags Remy inside the church doors, then runs down the stairs to the street to grab the chocolates. Inside the torn building, Remy's body lies on a pile of rubble that was once the gilded ceiling over the baptismal font. Eyes open, he sees nothing. There is nothing to see. Most of the ceiling is gone, roof beams balance on broken pews. The church's spires, now splintered, dry in the night air like chicken bones, the marrow sucked away.

In the street, Father Pascal tucks the chocolate box under his arm. The pink ribbon, now muddied and covered with Remy's blood, unravels a bit. God would not want waste at a time such as this, he tells himself, opens the box, stuffs a chocolate in his mouth. The bloodied ribbon falls into the street. The sweetness of the caramel makes his teeth ache.

Since the war began, Father Pascal has grown closer to the ground. His back arched. Marble films his eyes. The rectory, his books, all gone. All destroyed in the first assault. He sleeps in the sacristy, on tattered vestments rolled into a ball, like a stray dog. Drinks sacramental wine.

He closes the church door behind him. Bolts it, for no good reason. Puts another caramel into his mouth. "They are very good," he says to Remy's body, smiles, places the pink box on the flat of the dead man's stomach and begins to drag the body by its feet to into the sanctuary. "Very good, indeed." The round of his head itches. Sweat, like a skull cap.

All the while, Remy's eyes are open. Every now and then, Father Pascal catches the sightless stare, nods and smiles cordially, as if passing Remy in the street. "Such fine chocolates," he says. "Mmmm. Very nice."

At the end of this war, the body count will be 57,186,000. More or less.

12

THE CURTAINS ARE DRAWN. CANDLES LIGHT THE kitchen, quietly, as if by suggestion. On top of the wooden table, two glasses of cognac have been metered. The glasses are cut crystal, gold-rimmed. Incongruous in the stark room. The cognac bottle remains within reach. Mother Xavier throws another log into the brick oven. The oven door is open. The logs crackle and spit. Wood smoke curls like a cat. The air warm as skin.

Mother Xavier and Marie Claire are alone in the kitchen waiting for Anne. Marie Claire sits on a bench at the long chestnut table. The kitchen light frames her ivory face. A soft silk blouse, something Anne was saving from her previous life, folds around her, makes Mother Xavier think of the Sistine

Chapel, Michelangelo, the swaddling souls of the Last Judgment.

Anne is in the catacombs, looking for something for a child, something left behind, something, anything, so that she doesn't have to face Mother Xavier. Anne is too tired to discuss the rough edge of forgiveness. She only wants to sleep and dream of him, of them, at Le Madrigal, the warmth of his arms around her.

In the kitchen, Mother Xavier raises the flame under a pot of soup. Glances at the door several times. Without her glasses, she can barely see. She leans in close, too close. The blue flame flares. Her head is bare, tufts of hair singe. Lost in thought, she doesn't notice. She thinks of the Commander, the look of surprise, then fear. His body splashes into the river. His head hits the rocks. Jerks back. Hits them again.

The soup begins to boil, slowly. Pop after pop of white. The rhythm is the same. Hits the rocks, then back again, she thinks, pushes the image, the sound, from her mind. Tries to think about the soup as soup. It's hardly soup, though— potato, some dried milk—but it's more than Marie Claire has eaten for days. At least it's warm, she thinks. Steam forms a domestic halo around the nun's face.

At the kitchen table, Marie Claire is watching Mother Xavier intently and humming a song, "La ta-ta . . ." Spidering her fingers along with the music, a learned gesture. Mother Xavier recognizes the song is French, about a teddy bear. *Perhaps she learned it from her mother.*

I wonder if her mother had such beautiful skin, she thinks, like my mother, then pushes the thought back into the darkness. It's been so long since she's thought of her mother in that way, not the enemy, the moment pains her.

I must be tired. So very tired.

Marie Claire stops singing. "There's no need to be unhappy," she says, "That's what Monsieur Boubais said."

Mother Xavier stops her stirring. "And who is Monsieur Boubais?" she says, head cocked, leaning to one side like a trawler. "He sounds very wise."

Marie Claire seems confused. She looks at Mother Xavier as only a child can, astonished that an adult doesn't know the intimate details of her life. "He was to be my grandpapa," she says quietly. Speaks almost without breath.

Was.

The details are supplied by the tenor of Marie Claire's voice, its shadow. Mother Xavier looks at the small girl, closely, as if for the first time. Marie Claire is sitting up straight, like a good girl. Her black hair, wet, is neatly brushed, held back with a broad satin ribbon taken from one of Anne's chocolate boxes. Her eyes, like most children's, are shining. But unlike most girls her age, Marie Claire has a bearing, a dignity of carriage, that seems odd, older than her years.

Perhaps the child is in shock, she thinks.

"Are you hungry?" she asks.

Marie Claire shakes her head.

"How can you not be hungry?" Mother Xavier says, perplexed. "Children are always hungry. As a child, I was ravenous."

Marie Claire shrugs.

Mother Xavier's stomach rumbles like a storm, unfocused, angry. She wants sausage with plenty of garlic; fennel braised in chicken necks and thyme; jigged hare with figs and Camembert, ripe and runny with a gallon of Bordeaux. It's been more than a year since she's had a decent meal. White food is blinding, she thinks, makes her squint.

"Do the soldiers bring you bread?" Marie Claire asks.

"We make our own," Mother Xavier says, frowning. "It's very bad. Soft, no courage. Would you like some?"

Marie Claire pushes away from the table slightly. "No, thank you."

Mother Xavier moves in closer. "When was the last time you ate?" she asks, hands on hips.

"I don't know."

"Then you must be hungry." Mother Xavier taps her spoon on the metal stove. "Aren't you?"

Marie Claire says nothing, glances at the door, expectant.

Mother Xavier looks at her watch. The crystal is cracked, but it still runs. 7:30. *Where is Anne?*

"Are you ill?"

Marie Claire shakes her head.

Mother Xavier puts the spoon down, wipes her damp red hands on the apron of her habit. "Come here, let me see," she says, and places her hand on the girl's forehead.

"No fever."

She takes Marie Claire's wrist, feels her pulse. Steady. "Nothing hurts?" Marie Claire shakes her head again.

"How many fingers?"

"Two."

She is still not convinced that all is well, but the need to keep Marie Claire occupied, not staring at her in that odd, impossible, solemn way, outweighs Mother Xavier's sense of concern.

The child is fine. Tomorrow she will be gone.

"Well, then," she says, hands Marie Claire a stack of bowls. "Looks like you're healthy enough to set the table. The spoons are in the top drawer next to the sink."

Marie Claire carefully places the three heavy bowls on the table. Gold-rimmed, they, along with the cognac glasses, the cognac, the silver spoons, are the last of Le Madrigal. Anne's father delivered them to the convent hours before her uncle's restaurant became Central Command.

Mother Xavier, squinting to see, watches Marie Claire as she sets the table. She is looking for any sign of illness, exhaustion.

Perhaps the child is lying to us, not wishing to cause concern, she thinks. But finds it hard to imagine that Marie Claire is anything but the picture of health. In the darkened kitchen, the child's face glows amidst the candle flames, seems brighter than the flames themselves. So beautiful, Mother Xavier thinks.

"Is this right?" Marie Claire asks, straightens a soup spoon.

Mother Xavier swoops over the table, close like a bird. "Very nice, indeed," she says. Presses her watch up to her nose. 7:40. *Where is Anne?*

"Can't you see without your glasses?"

"Not really. I see you, but you shine like the candles if I look at you for too long."

Mother Xavier looks around the room, squinting, trying to evaluate the seriousness of the problem. "I suppose I'll have to get used to it," she says. The only thing she can clearly see are her own fingers spread in front of her face. She looks at them closely. "Where is my mind?" she says, and reaches into the pocket of her habit, pulls out a plain gold band. She holds it close to her face to see it clearly.

"Wedding band," she says. "We're all given these when we take our final vows. Married to God, you know. I never wear it when we leave the convent, in case we're caught. I don't want the soldiers to take it, sell it. They do that, you know."

The sight of the ring horrifies Marie Claire, but Mother Xavier doesn't notice. She kisses the ring, says a prayer of forgiveness, and places it on her finger.

"There," she says, "that feels better." She runs her hand through her hair, feels the singed edges. "Not again." She clucks, "Someday, I'll just go up in flames."

Marie Claire grabs Mother Xavier around the waist, hugs her tight. The fierceness of the gesture startles the nun.

"What's this?" she says, pulls the child's face close to hers.

Nearly nose to nose, she sees that Marie Claire's eyes are filled with tears. "It's all right," she says. "I only burnt a bit of my hair, no harm done."

Slowly, in the candlelight, Marie Claire reaches up and touches Mother Xavier's ring, then the bit of singed hair. Mother Xavier is amazed at how warm the child's fingers are, how soft, how gentle, how their touch makes her feel calm, somehow, serene, somehow.

Marie Claire says nothing. Her eyes are islands overgrown. Mother Xavier feels as if she is falling into the moment, as one falls into sleep, deeper and deeper, letting parts of herself go.

Marie Claire removes her hand.

The world sharpens again. Mother Xavier feels a profound sense of loneliness, as if the child's touch held within it a universe. She thinks again of the prophecy of Minouche. *The child saved is an angel of God.*

It cannot be, she thinks. There is something odd about this child, but Anne's mother was mad, not a prophet.

"We need napkins," she says. "There are some in the linen chest."

Without a word, Marie Claire opens the chest next to the cellar door. The sharp smell of cedar mingles with that of potato soup. She takes out three linen napkins. White on white, the shadow of lace.

"Do you know how to fold them?"

Marie Claire shakes her head.

"Here, give me one. I'll show you something Anne taught me. Her uncle owned a restaurant. Nice place. Very good food."

With nimble fingers, Mother Xavier pulls and pushes the bit of cloth, works the linen as if it were paper.

"It's a dove," she says, and hands the napkin to Marie Claire. "Isn't that nice?"

Marie Claire holds the linen dove in the flat of her hand as if it were a real bird. Kisses its head.

"Be careful now, the folds will come apart." *What is she doing? It's just a napkin.*

Marie Claire brushes the bird against her face.

Just then Mother Xavier notices the smell of burnt potatoes. "Oh my," she says, turns back to the stove. Squinting through the steam, she can see the soup is indeed burning. She turns down the flame.

"I should be more careful," she says. "God gives us so little food these days." With a large crooked spoon, she peels blackened potato from the bottom of the pot. "This isn't too bad though," she says, mostly to the soup. "Not too bad at all."

The soup, however, is badly burned. Sticks to the bottom of the pot, stubborn. It is all we have, she thinks, and wants to cry, thinks of a vichyssoise she once had in Paris. *How subtle the silk of leeks, the creamy potatoes.*

She holds back her tears and grinds the last bit of pepper into the pot. "There, it all looks like pepper now."

She turns back to Marie Claire.

In the candlelight of the kitchen, Mother Xavier thinks she sees the cloth wings of the dove move, ever so slowly, as if in flight. She squints harder, narrows the focus of her vision. The napkin still appears to be moving, appears to be a dove, hovering near the child's head. The Holy Ghost, Mother Xavier thinks. Crosses herself. The night presses in, the moisture of its cold breath, beads.

Marie Claire coos. It echoes as if the bird coos back.

Then stops.

The folds of the napkin fall away.

Mother Xavier is watching Marie Claire so intently that when the napkin falls open, her head jerks back, as if awakened from a dream. She watches the napkin fall to the ground, fall as any napkin would. Open. Square. Scatters the dust of the floor.

Mother Xavier walks over to it, bends to pick it up. It's just a napkin, she tells herself, I'm just exhausted, sniffs it as if to make sure. The cloth smells, not of cedar but rain and bark and the cool air of evening.

Footsteps in the hall. Anne's.

What should I tell her?

What is there to tell?

Nothing happened.

You're imagining things.

Although she hasn't smoked in years, Mother Xavier wants a cigarette and Arabic coffee, syrup thick with sugar, lots of sugar. White sugar, not brown.

Anne enters the kitchen. The dress she is holding is three sizes too large for the child. "It will keep you warm, at least," she says, standing in the doorway, hesitant to enter.

"Anne, come sit and eat," Mother Xavier says, sounding as calm as possible, "there's soup." *Things will be fine once we eat.*

Anne doesn't move. Won't meet Mother Xavier's eye. "I'm too tired," she says, edgy.

The room is shards, bare feet.

Mother Xavier pulls a chair out for Anne, says "Please."

Anne sits on the edge of the offered chair, looks at her hands.

So like her father, Mother Xavier thinks. *So many feelings inside of them, so difficult to get them out.*

With pot in hand, Mother Xavier fills the three bowls with soup. The nuns say grace, cross themselves, lift up their spoons but do not eat. Anne's body shudders, as if the air has suddenly been let out. Mother Xavier pulls her into her arms.

"How could he be the enemy?" Anne says, sobbing. Her body shakes. "How?"

Mother Xavier holds Anne tightly. *How is always the unanswerable.* She thinks of her own mother and father, a picture she has in her room. A formal portrait. She's just a baby, her parents, young, smiling, holding her toward the camera, so proud. On the back, in her mother's tight writing are the words, "You are so loved."

"Anne, we're going to have to leave here quickly."

Anne's body stiffens. "You said you thought he acted alone."

Mother Xavier studies Anne's eyes. The flecks of green, like fire, are gone. "Yes. I believe that," she says. "But if he suspected, surely someone else will. I think we're safe for tonight, but tomorrow morning . . ."

Mother Xavier coughs. Fine-grained like sandpaper.

Fear and apprehension hang in the air.

The quiet of the room is punctuated by the rhythm of Marie Claire's feet bouncing back and forth against the wooden bench. The metronome of childhood. So much is unclear to Anne. All she can think about is the wheat of his hair. Her father's fist.

Mother Xavier is silent, too. Thinking. *Ruth. The open palm. Unseeing. Are we next?* Mother Xavier looks at the child, so quiet. Perhaps she was wrong about Marie Claire, she thinks. In that moment, she looks like any child, but sadder. *Perhaps she is indeed in shock.* Mother Xavier feels herself soften to her. *So alone in a strange country, in the world.*

Mother Xavier raises her glass to the small child. "The World Needs Brave and Joyful Women of Faith," she says. "It was that motto that took me from being a schoolgirl on holiday with a friend to being the Mother Superior of this sacred order.

"No matter what happens, Marie Claire, no matter, remember us well," she says. "Remember us as filled with joy and bravery and always remember Anne, the one who saved you with her horns of white chocolate." Mother Xavier smiles, then laughs. Uneasy.

Anne runs her finger along the gold rim of the cognac glass. Raises it to the candlelight. "To Marie Claire," she says, her voice heavy with sorrow. To him, she thinks. To him.

13

THE STORY OF ANNE AND THE COMMANDER IS well known throughout the parish, but it is not the real story. She was not his whore. He did not use her. They did, however, meet by accident. That part is true.

He had spent the day painting a large canvas of St. Mark's— its towering spires, the dour saints that stood watch. It had always been a popular subject for artists. On any given day, a handful of easels sat in the shade of the striped awnings of the cafe Le Madrigal. When the Commander arrived in Tournai, he saw this, envied it, and found himself buying a set of oils.

There is no harm in painting again, he thought, but began to dream of the smell of linseed oil, the color and texture of the air itself. As each day passed, he found it increasingly difficult to complete the mission he was assigned. He was supposed to be sketching the river, the exact point where it intersected with a canal that led into the center of Tournai. A critical advantage point, if captured, and he knew it needed to be captured if they were to be successful.

But that day was warm. Kind, almost. "Germany will not mind," he thought, as he set up his easel in the early morning light. He knew otherwise, but pushed the sense of dread away, wondered why he had acquiesced to this, the life of the enemy.

He had come to think it was because he had no conviction. *All I had was my art and the doubt about my art. No love. No passion. No vision. Just skill and the fear of losing it.*

By the time the canvas was finished, the sun was already starting to set. Evening mass had begun. He checked his watch, 1800 hours, and thought of Claude Monet and his study of Rouen.

"Perhaps I shall paint this church every hour on the hour as Monet did his."

On the canvas, the sky he had rendered was vermilion, streaked with dust and warning.

He didn't see her coming. Anne was late, running full speed. Her red hair loose, wild in the wind. She turned the corner at Le Madrigal and her foot caught a chair. She slammed into his canvas and knocked it to the ground. The painting landed wet-side in the street. Before he could say anything, she grabbed it.

"I'm sorry, so sorry," she said, picking it up clumsily. She was out of breath. He noticed that her hands were streaked with paint. He was too stunned to speak. He took the canvas from her and held it at arm's length, silently assessing the damage.

"Please say something," Anne said and brushed her hair away from her face, several times, a nervous habit. The paint ran through the tangle of curls. Blue gray like the stone. The green of ivy.

He met her eye.

"I'm so sorry," she said again. Not knowing what else to say. The edges of the canvas had been reduced to a blur of muddy color. A veneer of dirt and rocks covered it all.

She expected him to be angry but the Commander moved from shock to amazement. As the sun set behind Anne, its golden light surrounded her face, the paint in her hair made her look as if she were wearing a crown. Of spring flowers, he thought. It reminded him of a painting by Peter Paul Rubens. The soft curve of her flesh, the kind, loving eyes.

"The Madonna in a Garland of Flowers," he said to her. He had seen it as a student at Alte Pinakothek in Munich. He and Anne were standing so close their lips could touch. "That's what you are. The Madonna. Your countryman Rubens has captured you well."

He moved a lock of hair from the corner of her mouth. Anne could hardly breathe.

"Forgive my boldness," he said. "It's just that you're so beautiful."

When she looked into his eyes, she saw her father's eyes. So much underneath the surface, she thought. *So much.*

I have to go, she said, and ran down the street and to the church. Took the steps two at a time.

14

THE CARDS TAPED TO THE WALLS OF ANNE'S room are blank. No greeting.

"Do you need some help?" she asks Marie Claire, who is fumbling with an undershirt she is trying to put on. The shirt is enormous compared to the child.

"No."

Marie Claire is struggling to put the shirt on, about to topple off of Anne's single bed. The candle Anne lit for her sheds little light. Flickers and spits.

"How can you see?"

Anne strikes a match and lights the oil lamp she uses for reading. The kerosene smokes. Marie Claire coughs just a bit.

"Let me help."

"I'm a big girl."

"Yes, you are," Anne says.

Marie Claire is determined. Anne can see that her head is poking through the armhole.

"I can get it," the child insists, wiggling out of the shirt, then tunneling back in.

"Fine."

I was probably that stubborn myself, Anne thinks, and picks up one of the many cards that have fallen off the wall in the child's wake.

"I'm getting a glass of water. Are you thirsty?"

Marie Claire shakes her head.

"Are you sure?"

She nods.

When Anne returns, Marie Claire is still struggling with the shirt. She tries not to watch, studies her walls instead.

How odd this must look.

No one has been in her room since she came to the convent. Anne never imagined what her cards look like to an outside eye. The bits of paper, tacked up haphazardly.

Even if the cards were to be mistaken for art, she thinks, disgusted, they are so simple-minded.

Anne walks from card to card shaking her head, picks them off the stone floor, embarrassed. The waving snowman with his Christmas greeting. The butter-soft chick wishing "A Joyous Easter!"

"That one's silly," Marie Claire says, finally tucked into the enormous shirt. She is pointing at a card tacked to the foot of the old wooden bed. The card swings back and forth on a rusted nail. It is the only card that Anne has not made. On its cover, a sophisticated cat wears a top hat, rakish in its angle. *Be mine!* The rouge cat is offering a ring. Instead of a diamond, a small sparkling fish.

"Yes," Anne says. "It's a very silly card." She holds the card in her hand and notices the colors have faded. The lines are not as skillfully drawn as she had first thought.

"Who is it for?" Marie Claire asks.

"I don't remember," Anne says, but most certainly does. She recalls the night in great detail, plays it over and over again in her head.

Her uncle watched them from the kitchen door. The Commander had ordered a bottle of champagne. He had painted this card for her. It's lovely, she said, but her voice gave away the disappointment. After all the weeks they had spent together, Anne had expected more than a card. Everyone in her family had expected more than a card. But a card was all he said he could give her, at least for now.

I will come back for you.

It looks like you, Anne told him. She didn't know what else to say. She ran her finger over the cat's face. Its clear blue eyes.

Believe me, he said. I will come back. Then he kissed her. You must promise to wait for me.

And if I don't? Anne said, trying to sound playful, trying to hide her anger, her tears.

He just looked away.

"I like this card," Marie Claire says.

"It's time for bed," Anne says. The smell of the bleached sheets suddenly makes her drowsy.

"Can I keep it?" the child asks.

Anne hesitates. *It's just a card. It isn't him.* "All right," she says. "If it will make you happy."

Marie Claire kisses the face of the cat, its crooked blue eyes, places it on the thin pillow. "I'll take good care of it." *It's all I have left.*

Marie Claire waves at the cat. "He's very pretty."

"Yes, he was," Anne says, distracted. *I will come back for you.* His voice was what she liked the most about him. It was clear and steady, like a bell. Tears run down her face.

"Don't cry," Marie Claire says. "He'll be back."

The words are like a slap. "What did you say?"

"Will you tell me a story?"

Anne pauses. *Did I hear her right?*

"Please?"

Marie Claire looks so helpless in the large shirt, Anne's heart breaks. *If only she were mine.* "Okay, get into bed," she says, suddenly tired, and pulls the blanket back for Marie Claire. "I must know a story. Something with princesses who live happily ever after."

An impossible story.

Marie Claire slides into bed but the silk undershirt wraps around her, tangling her up.

"I'm stuck."

Anne, smiling, shakes her head. Marie Claire is indeed stuck, *like a worm in a cocoon*. With one quick gesture, Anne lifts her into the air, over her head, and shakes her like a stick. Marie Claire giggles. The silk untangles. Anne laughs and sets her down gently.

"Take that off," she says, "before it strangles you."

Anne rummages through her dresser drawers. "Put this on," she says, and hands Marie Claire a small black sweater, like a doll's. Lamb's wool, handwoven. "It was mine before I washed it," Anne laughs. "It gets cold in here at night."

Marie Claire pulls the shrunken sweater over her head, but it's too small, even for her. Arms up, she is stuck, trying to squeeze her way into it.

"All right. All right. Let's try something else."

Anne pulls Marie Claire from the sweater's grip. The child stands unsteady on the bed. The lamplight, inconsistent as memory, shines across her frail naked body. In the dim light, Anne sees a bruise in the center of her bony chest. Large as a fist, it appears to be in the shape of a star.

"What is this?"

Wasn't there a minute ago.

Marie Claire's skin is cold, bumps under the warmth of the light. Anne looks closer, confused. She knows there was nothing there; not a minute ago, not an hour ago when Marie Claire was in the washtub.

"Did you fall?" Anne asks, but knows she didn't. Marie

Claire shakes her head. The sill of Anne's bedroom window rattles, startles Anne. "What's that?" she says, squints in the darkness but can see nothing, nothing except greeting cards moving back and forth like a hand slowly waving.

Marie Claire runs her finger along each point of the star. Slowly. The points rise from her skin like a birthmark. "Look," she says, reaches out and takes Anne's hand.

The Star of David, Anne thinks, and cups her hand over the girl's, tracing along the points with her. The star is warm to the touch. Marie Claire's breath rattles like wind, a broken fence.

"It's my heart," she says.

Anne notices a glow around the child, like the candle, the flame of the lantern. Her mouth goes dry. The smell of roses overwhelms her. She moves away, wants to run. Her mind a cyclone, heavy, low to the ground. Fear and reason, counterclockwise in the vortex of the moment.

On the floor, a box of chocolates, just opened, is empty. Lying by the foot of the bed.

I only left her in here for just a moment, she thinks. Then remembers what her mother had told her.

Chocolate is the one thing they cannot get in heaven.

The small paper cups tumble across the floor, empty.

15

FOUR A.M. THE COCK CROWS, IMPATIENT FOR A
new day. Anne has spent the night watching Marie Claire tumble in her sleep. Her dreams, swift clouds, pass over her face
and Marie Claire seems transformed within them. Their heat
brings forth the sheen of her skin, the horizon of her hair
resonant with darkness.

All night long, as Anne watched, she pressed the black beads
of her rosary, tightly. *Our Father. Hail Mary. Glory Be to The
Father. Announce the mystery; then say Our Father.* Her fingers
ache. Hundreds of words have been offered to God for guidance. The cock crows again. The inevitability of sunrise.

Outside the convent's walls, the city wakes. One by one,
rooms take spark, light the dark streets. But inside the convent
there is but one light. Across the courtyard Anne sees Mother

Xavier's room, and her chest goes tight, filled with a sudden sorrow. The worn comfort of monastic life, its gentle predictability itself a prayer, feels gone forever.

The child should sleep, Anne thinks, shuts the curtain, closes the door quietly behind her. She is going to the kitchen to pack some food. We must leave, she thinks, but wants her life back. 4:30 morning prayer. 5:30 first chores. 6:30 breakfast, a piece of bread, then three hours of labor. The life she knew as hers, unchanging as the sweetness of milk.

The outside air is heavy, expectant. The smell of rain is in the distance. Crossing the courtyard to the kitchen, Anne sees that the soldiers who usually watch the convent are gone. The street is empty. Outside the gate, its rusting iron bars, there is silence.

In the convent's kitchen, dishes sit unwashed in the sink. The curtains are drawn. On top of the wooden table, two glasses for cognac. Now empty. The bottle within reach.

Anne pours herself a drink. *Who is this child?* The cognac goes down in one swallow, burns. Her stomach is empty, the liquor warms her. She takes off her cornet, the wimple. Worn for more than three days without rest, it makes her head itch. *I wish there were time to bathe.* Her hair hangs heavy around her shoulders. She throws two logs into the brick oven, a bit of kindling. Lights it. The wood spits to life and fills the room with wood smoke.

She opens the kitchen window. The air has turned so cold,

she squints. The sky is strangely green. Storm clouds billow like smoke. Anne stands watching for a moment. Lightning flashes within the clouds. No rain yet but the wind picks up.

At least my hair, Anne thinks, and moves the dishes from the sink to the drain board. *I should have time for that.* She runs the cold water. The harsh smell of lye stings her eyes. It is the best we have, she tells herself. She runs her nails through her scalp. Thinks of warm tubs filled with lavender oil. Soap milled in Spain with goat's milk.

When her hair is finally clean it sticks together. She rubs it with a towel, hard.

"Is it morning, yet?" Marie Claire says, standing in the doorway.

"Nearly," Anne says, cautiously, half expecting something to happen, half dreading it. "I was just going to warm some milk." Anne takes out a saucepan and a pouch of dried milk. "Would you like some? We get them from the soldiers."

Mother Xavier enters the room. "They've come," she shouts. "I saw them from my window."

Anne and Marie Claire look out the window, the sun has inched higher, casting some light, but the clouds are darker, lower to the ground. Lightning connects. In the flash, Anne sees uniforms outside the gate, spilling into the street. A dozen or more. The Commander in the center, shouting orders.

"He's alive," Anne says. "He's not dead at all." Tears are streaming down her face. The rumble of thunder.

"But he's still the enemy," Mother Xavier says. "There are too many of them. We're trapped." She paces up and down. Picks up a butcher's knife for good measure.

"Maybe he won't hurt me."

Mother Xavier shakes her head. "He saw you with the child. Even if he didn't recognize you at the time, he'll figure that out as soon as he sees you dressed like this. He has no choice. He has to kill you."

The soldiers are wrapping a length of chain around the iron gate. Attaching it to the bumper of a munitions truck. Soon it will be over.

"What about the catacombs? We could try to climb up the coal chute," Anne says, but as soon as she speaks she knows it is impossible. The chute is long and steep, no footholds.

The soldiers run behind the convent. *They know.* Soon, they will slide down the chute, then run up the stairs to the kitchen.

We are surrounded.

"Shh," Marie Claire says, but the women do not hear. They are too busy watching the soldiers in the street. Illuminated by lightning, they look like figures in a newsreel.

Anne imagines her death, wonders how fast the bullet will hit; how it will feel when it tears into flesh; how the blood will fill the lungs, how they will stop breathing.

Marie Claire's eyes are fixed on a point beyond the two nuns, beyond the window, a point in the street, where the Commander is shouting orders.

Anne is dizzy. It's not that she's afraid of death, she tells herself, it's just that she does not want to die here. In this room. Without meaning. *Shot*. Would he really kill me? she thinks. *What if he doesn't recognize me?*

There is a soft light around Marie Claire. The air is dense. A hum. "Shh," she says again.

"It's all right, child," Mother Xavier says, turning away from the window. She sees that Marie Claire is covered in light. It sheets off her like rain. Blinding. "Oh, my God," Mother Xavier says. Falls to her knees.

Anne turns and sees that Marie Claire's hands are out-stretched, reaching for her. Anne wants to scream but can't. The light grows so bright she can't even finish her thought.

Outside, the gates of the convent moan, disappointed at their own weakness. The rusted bars tumble. The gate gives way.

Anne knows there is a simple explanation for this. Is desperately sure there is a simple explanation. Her pulse is too fast. *The refraction of morning light through the glass panes. The storm makes it more intense.*

The sun is indeed rising. Shining through the clouds so brightly it seems to heat the room, like a magnifying glass. Anne's eyes water. That's all it is, she thinks. *It's just the sunrise, reflected, mixed with fear.* Anne cannot move toward the child. She cannot move at all.

The light emanates from Marie Claire's hands. Her palms, out-turned. A small sun.

Outside the room, a chaos of voices. Footsteps, like a train. Not now, Anne thinks. *I'm not ready.*

The kitchen door opens. The Commander squints. He can't see. The women do not move. His men pile behind him. The women do not breathe.

"What is this?" he barks. His voice harsher than Anne remembers.

"Sunrise. Damn bright. Even with the storm. Nothing in here." He looks around the room. His eyes are bloodshot. Anne wants to run her hand along the smooth of his face, so battered by the fall into the river. Blood crusts the wheat of his hair.

I am sorry you are hurt, she thinks. You are the enemy, she thinks.

"They're gone," he curses, yells to the others. The door closes.

They are safe.

"Miraculously safe," Anne thinks.

But the smell of his sweat still lingers, twines with that of roses.

16

AS THE LIGHT STREAMS FROM HER HANDS, MARIE Claire is outside the moment, watching it from beyond the room. She looks down at her palms, unscathed. Pure light, voices within.

Bo-ruch A-toh Ado-noi E-lo-hei-nu.

Her mother's voice.

Shabos . . . Yom Ha-kipurim.

And then, her father's.

Marie Claire opens her mouth to reply, to say the words she has been taught, the words of atonement. She cannot.

Yom Ha-kipurim.

Their voices together. Like a river in a land, a continent away.

Marie Claire feels her heart push against the cage of her bones. She cannot breathe, barely think.

Shh. G—d will hear.

And then it's over.

17

MOTHER XAVIER IS FIXED ON THE CHILD AND joyous. She has always prayed for this moment.

God is not a fickle lover.

In her mind, she forms a checklist. She titles it "Possible Saints to Appear at This Moment." Saint Catherine Labore, she thinks.

Saint Catherine. On the night of July 18, Saint Vincent de Paul's feast, in 1830, a nun, Sister Catherine, swallowed a small piece of Saint Vincent's surplice, a relic, and fell asleep.

Her mind is processing the story so fast she thinks in images, not words. She sees Marie Claire as the child of the story, dressed in white, light streaming from her hands.

God has forgiven the sins of my birth, she thinks. My parents. Forgiven their lives.

Anne tells herself it's just a trick of the light. And luck. *Lots of luck.* But she knows her mother was right. The child saved is an angel of God, an angel who has come for her. Tears well in her eyes. Fear and nausea. She is a girl again, hiding again in the closet.

Don't let them find me.

She wants her father to protect her again, hold her close, like he did when she was a child. *Before I disappointed him.* Tears roll down her cheeks. She brushes them away quickly, remembers the way he used to hide chocolates for her in the pockets of his black wool coat. She is trying hard not to sob, not to show fear, but it is nearly impossible. She looks into the courtyard. Wipes the tears from her face with her sleeve. The rain has broken. The courtyard is traversed with the muddy rivers of the soldiers' footsteps. My fate is God's will, she thinks, but is unwilling to embrace it.

"They'll be back," she says. *We can still save ourselves. Fate can change.*

Mother Xavier says nothing. She is still unfocused. Gray and shapeless. Fragments of her past, her desires, her fears, spark each other. Bang in the fury of the moment.

Mother Xavier goes to Marie Claire. "Are you all right?" she says, and checks her pupils. Not dilated. No head trauma. Her hands, no scars, no burns. Marie Claire's skin is cold, clammy, but the child seems herself again, small.

Mother Xavier takes Anne by the arm. "You must take Marie Claire to your father. She is not safe here."

"But the factory," Anne says. "One of the workers may see us."

"The factory's been closed for quite a while," Mother Xavier says. "I'm sorry, I should have told you but your father swore me to secrecy. He didn't want you to worry."

"But the chocolates, they still come every week."

"Yes," Mother Xavier says. "He delivers them himself."

Confused, Anne feels the rooms spin around her. *How can the factory be closed?* She has come to imagine her father like a butterfly pinned under glass. Unchanged. In her mind, his shops are still bright with brass. Cool marble counters waiting for the return of the starched smiling women.

"Be careful," Mother Xavier says.

Outside, the rain picks up force, turns its fury on the convent, shakes the windows. The room is squeezed. Anne thinks of the nights that her father worked late. The burns on his arms from sugar.

"You'll be fine," Mother Xavier says, squeezes Anne's arm. She cannot look at her too closely, for fear of crying. Of changing her mind.

"Aren't you coming?"

"No," Mother Xavier says. "There's something I have to do."

Anne hesitates.

"It's better this way," Mother Xavier says. "Safer for you and the child."

But what about you? Anne thinks, but can see that Mother Xavier has made up her mind.

"Hurry, they'll be back," Mother Xavier says. Then speaks

to Anne, lovingly, as if she were her own child. "And get that hair out of your eyes," she says, pushing the wayward curls out of Anne's face with a gentle hand. "I don't know how you can see."

The gesture saddens Anne, the gentleness of it makes her long for the kind of mother she didn't have. A mother without angels, without demons, or both. She gathers her hair, winds it around itself, into a tight bun. A gesture she has made for years. With two metal pins, she secures it. The unruly, now obedient.

Anne takes a deep breath. *I will not cry.* "It's time," she says to Marie Claire, and takes her hand tentatively. It is flesh, she thinks, like that of any other child.

For a moment the three do not move. Anne stands in the echo of the storm, unsteady, unwilling to leave.

"Pray for me," Mother Xavier whispers, without fear. Her cornet starched like wings. Her sorrow, an open wound. An odd angel. She embraces Anne. Tears a bit of lace from the hem of Marie Claire's dress, makes the sign of the cross, closes her eyes, swallows it whole.

Anne feels her panic rise again.

Shh, God will hear.

Fate can change.

"Peace be with you," Mother Xavier says to the child. The kiss is wet with the salt of tears.

"And also with you," Marie Claire says.

Anne just looks away.

18

DEEP WITHIN THE CATACOMBS MOTHER XAVIER waits, waits as she has always dreamed of waiting, has always practiced waiting, surrounded by the things that remain, the fabric of the lives of those who have sacrificed everything for their God.

God has forgiven me, my parents. Heaven will be ours.

Upstairs, on the kitchen table, there are three letters. One is addressed to her parents. It holds no accusations. The penmanship is perfect.

I am sorry. That's all it says.

Another is addressed to the Commander. It explains the details of their deaths, the desires of each nun to be remembered by her family. Final farewells from her and Anne, all written by Mother Xavier's determined hand.

The third, final letter, was the most difficult to write. From Anne to the Commander. Mother Xavier could easily mimic the small looped lettering of Anne's handwriting but had no idea of what to write. She knew few details, only how they met. The nun had no idea of what men and women say to each other in cafes. She never heard enough to make sense of it all. She simply wrote "Remember" on the pale blue stationery and sprayed a bit of Shalimar from the bottle she had taken from Anne when she first came to the convent.

Below, in the catacombs, the air is so thick it is hard for Mother Xavier to breathe. All is musty, damp. The pots and pans, books, the dresses, a doll here and there—these things of an ordinary life, no longer needed, make a mountain. Mother Xavier sits above it all. Dozens of candles circle her, the suits, the shoes, the intimate, the mundane. The light of the candles is pure, glorious. This is like God's light, she thinks. Like stars tossed from the heavens. Soon, the heavens will be under her feet, each star a warm light, like a grain of sand. *Such joy*.

Mother Xavier takes the habits, the rosaries, prayer books, and shoes. Stacks them neatly in small piles outside the door. These are the things the soldiers will find. Their conclusion will be simple. Driven by fear, the last remaining members of the Sisters of His Divine and Most Sacred Blood took their own lives. As the Holy often do, she thinks. *There will be no doubt*. Like martyrs of the past, Mother Xavier, Anne, and the Sisters of His Divine and Most Sacred Blood will live in immortality.

At least, this is what she tells herself.

Sitting here, waiting, among the remnants of others' lives, Mother Xavier is relieved to know that the mystery of her death, the why and how of it, is over. This is her final task. Her final stumbling block, which keeps her here on this earth, always waiting, always distant from what she knows she truly needs.

It is almost over, she thinks, but does not pray. There is no need. God knows.

There is a scratching in the darkness. Rustling. Something is moving. Small, like a doubt. The candles are low to the ground, but she sees it. A rat is confused by the light, the glow of wax. It runs up her foot, her leg, and stops on her knee. Watches. Mother Xavier is not afraid, just surprised. Surprised by how gentle the rat seems, wants to touch it. Half an ear gone. Tufts of fur, bloodied. It seems confused, as if coming from battle. Rats are so misunderstood, she thinks. Its black eyes are small, darting. He is afraid, she thinks. Mother Xavier moves her hand toward it, gently.

Threatened, the rat hisses. Jumps. Runs behind the nun. Knocks over a candle. The wax spreads. Flames. Claws scatter away across the stone floor.

Mother Xavier is disappointed, wants to run after the rat but knows she'll never catch it. All she wanted was to touch it. *Why did it run?* Her heart beats faster. She closes her eyes and opens them, contemplating a prayer, but somehow, the formality of it belies a lack of intimacy. *That will not do.* She wants to speak to God directly, ask Him so much, but suddenly feels afraid.

The fire from the candle has spread. Mother Xavier watches it as it moves along the river of wax. Back and forth like a wave.

"I am not ready," she says to no one. The rat is gone. The sound of her own voice frightens her. Unsure. So close to having it all, she thinks, and yet, so afraid to give herself over to love, to the passion of divinity. Mother Xavier knows nothing of passion. There was no one before her God. No one whose kiss she can remember. No one at all.

Stay calm. She makes a list of the saints she knows and their wondrous lives. Saint Margaret of Clitherow, Saint Catherine Laboure. Perhaps, Marie Claire. The blessed. If she runs, she cannot join them. Mother Xavier knows that. Her palms sweat.

Behind Mother Xavier the flame catches a rag doll. The feet, the legs, the dress. A small cloth bear, its glass eyes rattle to the ground like dice.

She closes her eyes and places her head between her knees. The reality of the moment has finally caught her, shakes her. Smoke slips into lungs. She coughs. If she runs, God will not love her, she thinks. *I have no choice.*

"My God," she prays aloud, as Jesus had prayed to his father. She prays within the fire of love, rocking back and forth, holding on tight. "I am not worthy. Only say the word and I shall be healed." The words sound less grand when she speaks them. Less profound. Weak, somehow.

Another candle falls, gently. Its wax spills at her feet. Mother Xavier feels it splash onto her toes. The fire has now moved closer, closer.

Our Father who art in heaven, hallowed be thy name.

The arm of a coat takes the heat. Holds it.

Thy kingdom come, thy will be done, on Earth as it is in Heaven.

The flame rolls in great waves, through the coat, to a dress. Shimmers the threads. The heat is gentle. Takes the chill from the stone air of the catacomb.

Her eyes are closed. On the backs of her eyelids, she sees the flame. Warm. Smoke, like a hand, gray and kind, wraps itself around the nun. She coughs again.

She breathes deeply.

Clouds of ash rest within her lungs.

Beneath her, the wood of the trunk on which she is sitting grows warm from the heat. Painted morning glories vine along the trunk's brass locks. Their peeling heads tilt toward the sun. Inside the trunk: a white rose pressed in a diary; a prayer shawl; a menorah made of olive wood, carved by a man whose name is now forgotten.

Inside the trunk is what is left of a generation.

Above is the sound of so many boots.

Marie Claire saw this, she thinks, my death, the burning. She knew this would happen. With one hand Mother Xavier reaches out as if to touch the child. The gold ring on her finger.

Flames spike around her. Mother Xavier clutches the trunk's brass handles. The metal is hot, burns her palms. No stigmata, no divine light. No vision of The Blessed Virgin. All Mother Xavier can focus on is a need, a desire to breathe, breathe fresh air. The air of Germany. Of her youth.

The warm air that rushed over her and Sister Ruth, sunning themselves like twin seals. The sweet air that swept her along, her dog at her side, his brown eyes transfixed on her every move as if she were something more than herself. Mother Xavier wishes to breathe that air, its twine of lilac and grass.

When death finally comes, it comes as sleep. Mother Xavier had hoped for so much more.

19

In times of war, the line between "what is" and "what is no longer" becomes confused. The dead walk. The living rot away inch by inch.

Dreams are no longer necessary.

When Anne arrives home, all should not be as she left it. That is logical. Remy is dead. But in times of war, logic no longer applies.

Anne does not know this. Not yet, at least. She is running with Marie Claire across the field toward home. The storm covers their escape. The rain is blinding, cold, like needles on the skin. Her head is bare, her hair hangs free. Dressed in a coarse muslin slip, Anne runs wildly, without shoes. Her hair smells of lye and ice.

Mother Xavier made her leave her habit behind, Anne was

afraid to ask why. Her slip is soaked clear to her skin. There was no time to find anything else to wear. A rosary is wrapped around Anne's free hand. She couldn't leave it behind. Doesn't want to let it go, ever.

He will not forsake you, Mother Xavier said.

Please take someone else.

In the darkness of the storm, Anne feels as if she is a child again, running toward her father's home, to him, to safety. Marie Claire is running hard to keep up. Anne is afraid to touch her, to take her hand. She remembers her mother's prophecy, knows that an angel of God is to come for her. *Why is this happening to me?*

Anne looks back at the child and sees Marie Claire stumbling behind her, rain running down her face. She wants to lift her into her arms, hold her close, but she can't. She's too afraid.

The storm lights the moment like flare.

The house comes into focus sooner than expected. Seen through Anne's tears, it is foreign yet familiar. So much forgotten. The stone of its walls, blue-gray, taken from the quarries near the convent. The trellised roses that still wind their way, but the house has lost its dignity. No windows. Rain and birds—all are welcome. In the distance, the factory sits. Imposing. Shadows it all.

Anne sees a light in the kitchen. The rain is turning to mist, making the moment feel urgent. In the field, without the cover of rain, Anne knows they are exposed. But in the house, there could be soldiers.

Mother Xavier would know what to do.

Anne's stomach churns, unsure.

Marie Claire tugs at her hand. "It smells like chocolate," she says.

Anne notices it too, but the smell is small, not the huge clouds from the factory that she remembers. The front door of the house is open. Double doors, cracked barely an inch. Anne pushes gently. The smell of chocolate rushes over them.

Inside the hallway, Anne can see that the house is dark except for a slice of light, which has slipped from under the kitchen door and spills into the dining room.

"There," Marie Claire says and runs to the door.

Anne runs after her, catches her by the arm. "Wait," she whispers. Grabs the door before it creaks. Holds it in her hand, white-knuckled.

I'm not ready.

Anne opens the door, just a crack. Remy is there alone. His face is smaller than she remembers. His hair overgrown as weeds. His arms, less strong. On the kitchen table, Anne sees a pink chocolate box, a ribbon cast aside, the seal. There are chocolate molds everywhere and saucepans of chocolate and caramel burning on the stove. He does this for me, she thinks. *All this, just for me.*

Remy turns and sees the light reflected in Anne's watery eyes. His hand moves to cover the molds, as if to hide them. A reflex. Without words, Anne opens the door. She takes her father into her arms. Standing in the kitchen, in what was once her home, his bones, like chimes, are a harmony that completes her. I am sorry, she wants to say. I am sorry, he thinks.

They say nothing. Marie Claire watches.

When Remy regains himself, he pulls away gently. He adjusts the buttons of his vest. Polished brass. "There," he says.

Order is restored, Anne thinks.

"You must be hungry," he says to Anne. "You are perpetually hungry." The tenor of his voice is as always, formal. Fussy. Anne doesn't expect anything more than that, but his eyes seem different. They are softer than Anne remembers, more willing to meet hers.

Remy doesn't ask about Marie Claire. He doesn't even look at her.

So odd, Anne thinks, but is happy to be home. "Sit here by the stove, it will be warmer," she says to Marie Claire, and pulls out a kitchen chair for the girl to sit in. They are both drenched to the skin.

"You're dripping on my floor," Remy says, and takes an old pink blanket from the linen closet. Anne remembers it being on her bed when she was just a girl. The wool is worn and knotted in places but it is warm and smells of cedar. Anne wraps Marie Claire in the blanket.

"There you go," she says.

"And what about you?" Remy asks. "You're still making a mess." He takes a towel from the kitchen sink. "Sit," he says to Anne. A command.

"I'm fine," Anne says. *Safe.*

"Sit down," Remy says, his tone stern. He pulls out a chair for Anne to sit in. Anne hesitates. I'm not a child, she wants to say, but she is cold. And wet.

"I don't have all day," he says, on the verge of a smile.

He is enjoying this, Anne thinks. It's a game. *Our game.*

Remy taps the chair with his index finger.

Anne sits at her place at the table. Her old chair still wobbles left to right.

"Head down," Remy says. Marie Claire is smiling.

As if it is a painful duty, Anne puts her head down. The thick red hair hides her happiness. Remy throws the cotton towel over her head and dries her brusquely, as one would a wet dog. The tangled curls bounce, unruly, but finally dry. Remy wraps the towel around Anne's head, like a turban.

"There," he says. "May I make breakfast now?" Remy feigns a beleaguered look.

How many times have I seen this before? Anne thinks. *He is playing, not critical. Not angry. It's just a game.*

"That would be nice," she says, happy in the moment. A faux frown passes across Remy's face. Manners, she thinks. "Thank you," she says. "That would be very nice, Father."

Remy smiles, as if he is pleased that his daughter has finally learned something from him. "We must always be civilized," he says. Marie Claire nods her head in agreement.

"No one asked you," Anne says, and winks. Marie Claire giggles. Winks back. *A child again.*

Anne feels twelve years old. Her mother gone, Remy is

making her breakfast before he leaves for the factory. His efficient manner, the love that hides behind its walls. Anne watches as Remy takes the copper pan of chocolate off the blue flame, replaces it with cast iron. Butter sizzles. The edges of the eggs turn brown and lace. The click of the spatula against the black pan. *How long has it been since I've seen him?* Ten months, she thinks. *Too long.* As she speaks, nervous energy propels her. She races through the story: the child buried; the reflected light of dawn. There are too many things to say. The words bump and jostle each other, slide off course. Such luck, she says.

"Who would believe it?"

There is no talk of miracles.

Marie Claire says nothing. Kicks the legs of her chair.

Remy sets a single plate for Anne. Pours coffee. Thick, no cream. Says nothing about the fantastic tale she has told.

Perhaps, he thinks me delusional.

"Don't you think it all seems odd?" Anne asks.

"No," Remy says, sits. Adjusts the pleat in his pants. Crosses his legs.

"No, that's all you can say?" Anne says. "No?" She is eating so quickly she barely chews. *This is so good.* Anne is hungrier than she thought, can't remember the last time she ate. She offers Marie Claire some egg, a bit of yolk. It slips off the edge of bread, falls onto the table, untouched.

"You have to eat something," she says. Marie Claire shakes

her head. "Please," Anne says. She smoothes a strand of the girl's hair.

"Here," Remy says, stands, takes a block of chocolate from the stove. Hands it to Marie Claire, who smiles.

"Chocolate is all they really want," he says to Anne. Looks at her with cinder eyes.

The grease of the eggs makes her queasy.

He knows.

She pushes the plate away.

"Now, you should get some sleep," Remy says, kisses her on the forehead, takes her plate to the sink. Anne doesn't move. She watches him closely. He rolls up his sleeves and begins scrubbing the cast-iron pan. "I'll get this," he says.

How can he know?

Her chest tightens. She can hardly speak. She pushes away from the table, from Marie Claire, and stands. He is only an arm's length away. She can smell his skin, the sweat and burnt chocolate. She wants to touch him, to see if he's a dream, perhaps this all is a dream, but she's afraid to.

"Go on," he says over his shoulder. "Up to your room." His voice is so casual.

"Father," she says, moves closer, puts a hand on his back. His body stiffens. She leans into him. "Don't let them take me," she whispers. Hoarse. She doesn't want Marie Claire to hear. "I'm not ready."

Remy doesn't turn around. Scrubs the pan harder. "I think

you should get some sleep," he says, his voice tired. "It's time for you to rest."

"Please," she whispers into his ear, puts her arms around him. "Don't let them."

They stand like this for a moment. Anne wraps her arms around his chest. Her head against his back. She can feel him breathing. His quick breath. His steady heart.

"Go on," he says, but doesn't turn around. Doesn't push her away.

His tears fall onto her hands, roll down her fingers.

20

ANNE HAD NO CHOICE BUT TO LET GO OF HIM, let her arms fall away, grow cold again. She is a dutiful daughter, she tells herself. Wishes it wasn't so. For whatever reason, it is her father's wish that she sleep. So, she will sleep.

What is unspoken between them remains unspoken.

As Anne slowly closes the kitchen door behind her, the sight of Remy and Marie Claire together, the child eating while Remy washes dishes, is so domestic it's nearly impossible to think of miracles. But she does. Asleep in her own room, excerpts from *The Lives of the Saints* run through her head. Catherine and the wheel. Joan burning at the stake. *Who was the one who died in the iron maiden?* Anne's body sweats. She lies on a sour mattress on the floor. Her bed, its lace canopy, is gone. The windows, toothless. Everything is matchsticks.

It's nearly supper when Anne finally wakes and enters the kitchen again. The room feels slant-eyed and trembling. Anne is confused. The room is filled with doves, fifty or more. She is afraid to count. The cooing of their incongruous music. The swoops of down. Indigo and the gray of far-off thunder. Like storm clouds, low, rumbling, dark-bellied: the doves provide their own current, part and tumble at will. In the center of all is Mother Xavier. Cackling, joyous, more joyous than Anne has ever seen her. The doves, thin-beaked, seem to hold her council. Sit squat on her crooked shoulders and whisper, as if she is a telegraph pole and they merely tired.

The nun laughs with them, shaking her head from side to side, in the tango of some private joke. Anne is embarrassed by her own presence, as if she has walked into someone else's dream and is not only unnecessary, but unnoticed.

Marie Claire and Remy sit at the kitchen table, genial as tea, speaking rapidly in a language Anne does not understand. They do not look up when she enters. In fact, no one seems to see her at all.

"Are you all right?" Anne asks Mother Xavier. Her voice, awkward, a schoolgirl's. There are so many questions to ask, so many which have no answer, she thinks.

"Peace be with you," Mother Xavier says.

"And also with you, Mother Xavier," Anne says, but knows the words seem unnecessary. She is indeed peaceful. The birds take flight. Mother Xavier dusts her shoulders. Small gray feathers fall onto the tile floor.

Mother Xavier moves closer, embraces Anne. Holds her with both arms and speaks in her Sacred Prayer Voice. Strong. Loud. Operatic in flight. *"Denn also hat Gott die Welt geliebt, daß er seinen eingebornen Sohn gab, auf daß alle, die an ihn glauben, nicht verloren werden, sondern das ewige Leben haben."*

John 3:16. She has never heard Mother Xavier speak German before. The word "God" sounds thunderous. The promise of everlasting life feels like a statement without compromise, but not without sorrow.

"I've come for the child," she says to Anne.

A few remaining doves beat their wings, low. Anne nods. Marie Claire takes Mother Xavier's hand.

"It's best this way, Anne," her father says, sipping from a cracked china cup.

The child is radiant, filled with the hum of light. Anne knows she should feel sad. Knows she is losing this child, probably forever, but does not cry. Marie Claire turns away, just for a moment, and then rushes into Anne's arms, hugs her neck. The smell of roses is overwhelming.

"Who are you?" Anne whispers.

"Do not be afraid," she replies.

Outside, the air moves, a swift current, suddenly filled with the beating of wings.

21

THE COMMANDER TAKES ANNE'S ROOM IN THE convent for himself. The tiny room he has chosen provides a clear view into the courtyard and the river beyond the convent's walls. A perfect site for surveillance. *Perfect and warm.*

He has no idea this was Anne's room. One room looks so much like the other. Cluttered with the lives of others. Nothing, anywhere, reminds him of her. All he can think of is sleep. He and his troops are tired of sleeping in the mud of the camp, without proper food or heat. The convent will serve us well, he thinks. Holds his head in both of his hands. The room is spinning. He sits down on the narrow bed.

He wants to be pleased with what has unfolded. The convent is now in his control, his men now have a decent place to stay, and the Resistance no longer has a hold in Tournai.

Berlin will favor him once more. This is what he had wanted, but now that it has happened, he knows this is not what he wanted at all. Not this way.

Anne.

He looks around the room. Bits of paper are everywhere. A snowman laughing.

What form of worship is this?

He coughs. Spits blood into his neatly folded handkerchief. Not just a little. He tries not to think about it. Tries not to give in to the pain that ebbs and flows. Since his fall, he has been unwell. A broken rib, undiscovered, rubs against his heart like a match. He is sweating from the heat of his own body, 104 or 105 degrees. He can't seem to drink enough water. Can barely focus his eyes. Only wants to sleep. Just sleep.

He picks up a card that has fallen on the floor. *"Je t'aime."* He knows enough French to know it speaks of love. To whom is in question. *"Je t'aime."* The menu at Le Madrigal was in French. That first time she had helped him order. His French was so bad he would not even speak it. There was something about her red hair, the way it always seemed surprised, that intrigued him. The calm eyes, the peak of her lips. Nothing was casual about her, every word so heartfelt, impassioned.

From his pocket, he takes the blue letter left for him on the kitchen table. The blue paper. The smell of Shalimar. "Remember."

How could she take her life?

He runs a hand through his hair, so tired. He imagines his

eyes are rimmed, bloodshot. His coughing persists. The smell of burnt hair, flesh, sticks to him. He has decided that he will not force his men to go through the ashes. What remains is proof enough. The neat stacks of clothing. The notes of farewell.

When he picked up the letter to M. Mathot, something inside of him shut down.

Love is the pastime of fools.

He always suspected the old man lied to him; suspected that Anne was alive, but to have lived so close to her for all this time, so close, and yet, in the end, not being able to save her, was more than he could bear.

Did she fear me, or what I had become?

He pushes the thought away. My clothes will have to be destroyed, he thinks. Slowly, the Commander stands, removes his Luger, its holster, his uniform. The scratch of wool makes him itch. His undershirt is ringed with sweat and yellowed. Around his neck is a medal hanging from a blue cord. It is the Blessed Virgin, standing on a rock. Her hands outstretched; stars form a halo. She is at peace. Around her sacred body are the words, "O Mary Conceived Without Sin Pray For Us Who Have Recourse To Thee."

The Commander was given the medal at his first Holy Communion and has worn it ever since. The Miraculous Medal, it is called. His parish priest told him that the medal is indeed miraculous. It cures insanity, leprosy, and has the power to convert hardened sinners, such as Jews, unbelievers, and Free-masons.

Every month, the priest sends the Commander a dozen or more of these. "Do this in memory of me," he writes on a small card. An encouragement. A quote from the mass, the taking of Christ's body. The medals jingle in the Commander's pockets like spare change. When he can, he slips them over the necks of dying Jews, wipes the blood from his hands, and prays for his own salvation.

In the darkness of Anne's room, he fingers the medal around his neck and prays, once more, by rote, as he has prayed so many nights before. The letter he is to deliver to Mother Xavier's parents sits beside him on the single bed. His prayer finished, he picks it up and holds it. The smell of charred flesh overwhelms him.

He has a sudden urge to slap Mother Xavier hard. See the welt of his hand across her face. He knows the Kepplers had written their daughter of their arrival. *They are good people, loyal to the cause.* Not deserving of such betrayal.

The Commander falls back on the bed. The hacking cough begins again. Blood stains the sheets. A card over his head flutters.

. . . pour la Nouvelle Année!

Something about a Happy New Year.

He doesn't look forward to tomorrow and the Kepplers' visit. He tosses their letter onto the floor.

Je t'aime.

The letter slips under the bed, next to a card, a card of love. A cat in a top hat offers a fish instead of a ring. *Be mine!* he says with crooked blue eyes.

When the Commander finally sleeps, he sleeps fitfully, dreams of what he will say to the Kepplers, but in French, a language he barely understands, speaks badly. He dreams of that, and a tangle of red hair.

22

"WE MUST BE ALMOST THERE," MOTHER XAVIER says to Marie Claire.

Marie Claire nods.

The two are on a train. The countryside slips by like moonlight across marble, rocks gently from side to side. Marie Claire shifts in her seat, uneasy. Mother Xavier rattles along, a violin, discordant. A train is not what she expected.

Marie Claire takes a piece of chocolate from her pocket. It is carefully wrapped in pink tissue. A parting gift from Remy. She offers some to Mother Xavier, who eats it greedily. There is no one else in the compartment. It is worn slender. Threadbare velvet. Mahogany, stained with the oil from the skin of hundreds. The wheels of the train, like broken glass, spark against the tracks, light the night for only a second, then fade into the background of what has been.

The train picks up speed. To Mother Xavier, it is seemingly destinationless, and yet filled with intent. The train sparks and squeals along. Headstrong. Its howl, the wail of its whistle, an erratic pulse. Mother Xavier notices that the landscape outside the window shifts, so slowly, like a bit of smoke. It looks like France, but not the France Mother Xavier knows. And yet, somehow it is familiar. She knows this place. She can feel it in a way she has never felt anything before. A vise. Her breath is short.

Is this heaven?

Marie Claire eats her chocolate and kicks her feet along with the rhythm of the engine. The sound vibrates within the nun. There is something else, something, a back beat, an undertone, something underneath the sound of the engine, the surge of its power. A word.

Gahelet.

Even though they are alone, she hears it over and over again. In the voices of men, women, children, the aged and the strong. There is no one else on the train. It is not German, not French or Flemish.

Gahelet.

Hundreds of voices. The child kicks her feet harder, back and forth.

"Marie Claire, please. Do not kick like that," Mother Xavier says.

"Gahelet means embers," Marie Claire says, and takes another bite of chocolate. The train jerks around a bend, then through a tunnel. All is dark, dark as remembering.

Embers.

The sound of the voices, the train, eases out of the turn, falls out of time. The compartment lights flicker. They have arrived. The train doors open with billows of steam. Mother Xavier takes Marie Claire by the hand, unsure of where to go—unsure if this is a dream, or if death is merely a station in which one waits.

It is a place without wind.

There are no conductors, no baggage. Only a platform. Mother Xavier looks back at the train. Behind their passenger car is a line of cattle cars, snaking far as the eye can see, heavy with snow. They back into the darkness of the tunnel from which they came. The doors of the cars are open.

Mother Xavier moves closer, holding Marie Claire with the sweat of her hand. The lights of the station, small moons, pool upon the slat wooden floors of the open cars. Their hollowness draws her closer. There is something on the floor, not dust, darker. Mother Xavier runs her fingers along the awkward wood.

Gahelet, she thinks.

She takes her fingers to her lips. The taste is familiar, slightly sweet. She does not swallow.

The body of Christ.

Somewhere within this moment, Marie Claire slips away.

Mother Xavier is not sure when the child let go of her hand and left. Time is becoming elongated. In the distance, she notices a city, its squat buildings scattered in barbed wire, tossed like so many pieces to a puzzle. A series of smokestacks on the outskirts. A factory, of some sort. Billows of smoke in the graying sky.

Where is heaven?

The ashes on her tongue burn.

23

THERE ARE SO MANY QUESTIONS BETWEEN THEM
that Anne is afraid to speak. Answers will change everything.
Right now, the moment is simple. She is Remy's daughter.
He is her father. Nothing else is as true as that.

Remy stirs the copper pot. His wooden spoon clicks against
the pure ceramic liner.

"If it heats too quickly, it will turn bitter."

Remy has never taught Anne his craft before. The appren-
ticeship makes her happy but afraid that she won't please him.
She holds the spoon carefully. Stirs slowly, as her father in-
structs.

"To understand chocolate is to understand life," Remy says.
He fingers his recipes, stained and brittle, as one tests the finest
of fabric. Gently rolls them between finger and thumb. As the

hours pass, he teaches Anne the mysteries of chocolate: its unruly temperament, its haughty disregard for the science which rules it.

"Sometimes, like the heart, I think it just desires to burn," Remy shakes his head, cleaning the pot, its blackened sugar edge.

All around them the house is a shock of timber and glass. The doves are gone. Crows fly through the living room, and yet, within the kitchen, which Remy never seems to leave, all is as Anne remembers. Yes, the windows are gone, but the stove, burnished silver, six burners, is blue with flame. The rows of copper pots squint in the morning light. The marble of the counters is still cool to the touch. The larder pushes at its seams with eggs and butter and the sweetest of cream. Nothing has changed and yet everything has changed. Still, with each passing moment, Anne grows more happy than afraid. There is an easiness between them now, an unspoken gentleness.

Hours go by, Anne and Remy work side by side, filling the pink boxes. Tying them with ribbons. The table is filled with their work, as is half the kitchen floor. The packages make walking difficult, but there is no talk of delivery.

"It's late," Remy says. Points out the window. A shower of meteors, their eerie tails, moves unhurried. "Why don't you get some sleep?" he says.

Anne is tired but afraid to leave the kitchen. She knows that reality shifts around her now, unencumbered by logic. He will not be here if I leave, she thinks. Covering herself with her old pink blanket, Anne sleeps in the corner of the kitchen dreaming a wild mosaic of emotions, not dreams. At one point, she thinks she's cried out. Remy kisses her head, wipes her brow with his monogrammed silk handkerchief, which she takes, clutches in her fist.

I am sorry, she thinks he says; he kisses her again. I am so very sorry I could not love you better. The words run through her like a current.

Anne is still asleep as the pilots enter their planes, pull their goggles over their eyes, buckle themselves tightly into their seats. When they start their engines, her body jerks awake. The kitchen is open to the world, like a heart. The roof is gone. Anne can see that Cassiopeia points toward the North Star.

She sits up, looks around the room. There are no boxes, no gay ribbons. No chocolates. The stove, toppled over on its side. Was I dreaming? she wonders, unclenches her hand, slowly.

No. No dream.

In her palm, a perfect handkerchief, clean and starched, like a single rose. Her father's initials, "R. M.," twine like ivy.

When the air-raid sirens begin, their howl is low and dark and crests through Anne's body, the people of the city, the dogs and cats they care for. What is left of Tournai goes underground to the shelters. They bring clear water, ther-moses of coffee and wine. A birthday cake with candles. The last bit of cheese. The children bring their schoolbooks. Life, even in war, must go on.

Anne does not move. Lying in the rubble of her father's house, she takes no shelter. *There is no need.* She has nothing left. Nothing, except the handkerchief she holds to her lips. The initials "R. M."

Above her head, the gray and green of the fighter pilots.

When they come, they come like crows, but darker.

24

WHEN MOTHER XAVIER SEES HER PARENTS, SHE IS surprised. They are standing in the rubble of what she thinks was once Marie Claire's village, taking notes.

How did I get here?

She thought she was walking toward the city, with its factory and smokestacks, but the closer she came to it, the more it faded from view. Soon, she found herself amidst bones and bricks. Marie Claire's house stands off in the distance. The moon is cloaked in the gauze of dusk.

Her mother's laughter rings clear, a precise bell.

It's been many years since she's seen her parents. So many, she can't remember exactly how long it's been. She waves and calls out. They can't hear her. They are still lean, hardly damaged by age.

The Kepplers have not yet been to the convent, not yet seen the letter that bears their name. The perfect handwriting waiting to be read, patient. Her mother is still happy. It is her intent to move their facility near Tournai, so they can be closer to their only child.

"It is time she forgives us," she told her husband. "We are not barbarians, what we do we do for science. To achieve perfection. Is that not the goal of religion also? The necessary suffering, the struggle for perfection?"

Her husband had no choice but to agree. It was the right decision on many levels. Yes, they would be able to reestablish their ties with their daughter, but, more importantly, there'd been an incident. They need a place where they can continue their work unnoticed.

A young officer, a medical student assigned to assist them, had filed a complaint against the Kepplers. After working with them for only a short time, the officer charged that their experiments were unnecessary, dangerous to the troops and, perhaps, even Germany.

"Nonsense," Herr Keppler said when he first heard of the grievance. "It's a simple procedure."

Written down with a clinical eye, their reports, their work, did, indeed, seem simple.

Thirty children were gathered from the trains as they arrived. The taller the better, preferably with broad shoulders, strong hands. Once chosen, they were brought to the facility, strapped down on thirty beds.

This was the most difficult part, they wrote. Although the prisoners hadn't eaten for days, they, being children, still had a reserve of energy, a tendency to struggle, to ask questions.

The Kepplers waited in their office until the subjects were prepared. "Objectivity must be maintained."

When ready, ten male children received 10 cc of Vogan into the palm of their right hand and the interior surface of the forearm; ten females eight drops directly into both left and right eyes; and the rest of them, nothing.

The officer was only required to record the prisoners' reactions, take photographs, and be careful not to stand too near.

"What could be more simple than that?" Herr Keppler asked his wife in disbelief. "The man is an imbecile."

"The problems began right away," the officer wrote in his complaint. "As soon as the children had contact with Vogan, their bodies were covered in burns. The blood literally boiled beneath the skin. The boils would burst, covering my face, my hands.

"At midnight, I went to bed. The next day I realized I couldn't see."

The officer reported that his blindness was temporary, however, and a week later he recovered most of his vision.

"When I could finally see again, I was summoned by the Kepplers to return to the experiment, not to help the children, but to photograph them. From this day forward, I was to photograph them every day, but no one took care of them; they were screaming like animals.

"Soon," he wrote, "the children had lost all reason, scream-ing, clawing, like so many rats, on the edge of insanity."

Within the complaint, the officer enclosed duplicate prints of the children. Wild-eyed. Skinless as rats.

"It should be added," he wrote, "if one wishes to radically alter genes, then these experiments could just as well have been carried out on animals, or on plants, as with the work of Mendel. It seemed to me, since I had often seen the Kep-plers standing quietly in the chaos of the room watching the pain of these children with the calm, calculating stare of a hawk, that it was, for them, more exciting to experiment on humans."

The officer's report had been forwarded to the Kepplers from Central Command with a note written across the top.

"Officially, you no longer exist," it said.

The Kepplers had no choice but to relocate.

Mother Xavier knows nothing of her parents' plans—only of their visit, their wish to speak to her. The closer she walks to them, the more she sees how they've aged. Their voices, taut. The air around them is thick with flies, an incessant buzz. Her father turns toward her.

"Look," he says. "Birds. A field of them. They seem to be hovering, not flying."

He is pointing just beyond the place where Mother Xavier stands. For a moment, it seemed as if he was pointing at her. She felt the color rise in her face, thought of the photo that she had left in her room. Her mother and father, so young, so happy. She, just an infant. The inscription. *So loved.*

Her mother turns for just a moment, "Those can't be birds," she says. "Birds don't hover."

Mother Xavier turns. Indeed behind her there appears to be a field filled with small black birds. Their bruised eyes. They are tangled in a thatch of glass and what seems, from that distance, to be wood, charred.

"Let's take a look," he says. Mother Xavier can see the flash of his gray eyes. Their spark.

"Come on, where's your sense of adventure?"

Her mother taps at the face of her watch and frowns. Her hair is more gray now than brown. Cut like a man's, its waves catch the last light of day. "We don't have time," she says. "The driver is coming back for us any minute."

A frown passes over her father's face for just a moment, then he begins to run. "Come on," he says, over his shoulder. "We'll hurry then."

Despite his age, he is quick. A sleek runner, the product of many years of physical training. Mother Xavier follows behind. She can barely keep up. Her mother passes her, laughing.

"You are such a fool!" she shouts.

Mother Xavier smells the heat of her mother's body, the antiseptic mixed with sweat. A smell she remembers from her childhood.

Her father reaches the field first, beats them both, so handily. For a moment he is young again, triumphant. Then, he falls to his knees. "My God," he says. "These are not birds at all."

"What is it?" her mother says. She has been running but is not out of breath. "The smell is so bad, I can hardly see."

Mother Xavier stands behind her, a shadow.

"The impossible," her father says. Quick, excited. The field is filled with irises, black, big as a man's fist. "I've never seen anything like this before."

There are dozens and dozens of bulbs scattered among the tangle of hands and feet, some of which are burned to embers. Flies make their way to the bone. The irises are growing tall and upright.

Her mother runs a finger along a dark petal. "The embers must serve as fertilizer, these plants are so healthy they grow without soil, without root."

Gahelet.

Mother Xavier turns away. She can no longer bear it.

"They're some sort of hybrid. All this glass, there must have been a greenhouse here."

Her father gently digs at an iris. The bulb is growing between an arm and a wayward foot. Two toes missing. Blood covers his hand.

"Yes. Yes, I think you're right," he says as he digs, his fingernails black. The mud. "Hybrid work, that would explain it . . ." The iris finally gives way.

"There, very nice. A perfect specimen."

His wife takes the iris from him and inspects it gently, the silk of its petals, its sharp stem. "The genetic code is altered profoundly," she says. "I've never seen anything like it."

Herr Keppler wipes the blood from his hands on a dress in the pile. The pattern of small roses. "And what is this?" he says. Next to the dress is a black leather notebook. He picks it up. The wind catches its pages. The Xs and Ys. The work of Mendel and more.

"Very good. Very good indeed." he says, and smiles. "Certainly less strenuous than children."

25

MARIE CLAIRE DIDN'T MEAN TO LET GO OF Mother Xavier's hand, but it was time for her to leave.

This is all that can be assumed. This, and that Grandmama Paulette would have been very pleased. The iris will continue. Big as a man's fist. Blue black. The color of Marie Claire's hair.

26

No moon. The stars look away. A lamp is lit in the convent's kitchen. There, the Commander, unseeing, looks out into the dark night, into the river. Its secrets. The kitchen light casts a shadow. It scatters down the hill, fades into the waters below. He coughs hard. The room spins.

The need for sleep is overwhelming, but every time he lies in Anne's bed he feels himself fall into a dream, a flying dream. He is pulled backward through the air, through the clouds.

And then he wakes up.

The Commander picks up a glass from the unwashed pile in the sink. Sniffs it. The caramel sweetness of cognac. He pumps the water, hard but not hard enough. Doesn't notice when Anne enters the room. She is dressed once more in her habit. The horns of white chocolate.

In la sua volontà è nostra pace, she says to him, touching his shoulder.

At first, he thinks she is a delusion. His temperature burns away at his brain. He continues to pump for water. Harder. It rushes into his glass, rust-brown and then clear. He takes a sip.

"*In la sua volontà è nostra pace*," she says again. Her hand caresses the back of his neck.

It is nothing, he thinks, and coughs until the coughing becomes uncontrollable, the blood overwhelming. The glass slips from his hand. Breaks on the floor.

"I am still sleeping," he says, choking the words. "Just sleeping."

Anne takes him into her arms.

In la sua volontà è nostra pace.

The words seem louder this time, as if they have somehow become a part of him, like air, like blood. Anne's lips press against his cheek.

In la sua volontà è nostra pace.

He feels the words resonate. The phrase is familiar to him. *Latin, of course.*

Anne's arms are around him, he notices his coughing has stopped.

In la sua volontà è nostra pace.

The blood in his mouth has receded.

In la sua volontà è nostra pace.

The pain is gone.

In la sua volontà è nostra pace.

For a moment he is calm, he moves to kiss her lips, her lips, wild berries, overripe.

"*In la sua volontà è nostra pace,*" he says, finally remembering the meaning of the phrase, but when he speaks the words they sound more like a plea than a prayer, sound more like the words of a child who fears a promise is forgotten.

In la sua volontà è nostra pace.

In His will is our peace.

These are the last words he will speak in this world. Anne's lips are cool to the touch.

27

AFTER THE LIBERATION, THE REPORTS OF ANNE were numerous in Tournai. In one account, a man says the postulate saved his entire family. The air-raid sirens had gone off. They were hiding in a shelter when she appeared, saying the shelter was unsafe. She led them out into the night. The shelter was destroyed in the raid. The man and his family were saved.

"At the time, I didn't know she had been killed," he told the reporter. "She looked like any other person. Alive, well. And very kind. My daughter was quite frightened, but she calmed her with the story of another little girl. A Jew, a child, she had saved.

"The child saved was an angel of God, she told us.

"I remember with some shame, I said, 'But the child was a Jew. How can she be an angel of God?'

"She turned to me, as if I had struck her. 'That is the question you must ask yourself,' she said. 'How is that possible?' "

The man then showed the reporter a photograph he had taken for a keepsake. "I had no idea," he said. "She looked as alive as you or me."

The photograph was clear, crisply rendered in black and white. Standing in a circle, there was the man, his wife, three children—all smiling. In the center of the group there was a shadow. If you looked closely at the blurred image you could see a nun, tall as a man, wearing a cornet that seemed on the verge of flight. On the edge of the frame, another figure stood. A man. The brass buttons of his striped vest. The perfect waves of silver hair. A father's proud smile.

"God has returned to us!" the headline read.

Perhaps.

Perhaps, He had been there all along.

ACKNOWLEDGMENTS

MANY THANKS TO THE BUSH AND HEEKIN FOUN-dations, whose financial support made work on this novel possible, and to the M.F.A. program at Hamline University, where this project began. In addition, special thanks to Francis Ford Coppola, his staff, and the members of the *Zoetrope All Story* on-line workshop for the opportunity to develop sections of this work in a supportive, critical environment. Thanks also to Liliane Opsomer of the Belgian Tourist Office for her help in the research stage of this book. I'd like to acknowledge the hardworking staffs and generous foundations that support the artist retreats at New York Mills, the Anderson Center, and Ragdale, where the bulk of this novel was fine-tuned. Special thanks also to my editor, Peternelle van Arsdale, for her keen eye and instinct, and my tenacious agent, Jo Fagan, for the support that kept me going. My deepest gratitude to my mother, Gisele Brandt, who encouraged me to write as soon as I could pick up a pencil; Sally and George Kelby, my favorite cheerleaders; and Stewart O'Nan for his unfailing encouragement and gracious heart.